**P9-CAT-701**

# S.S. SAN PEDRO
*and*
# CASTAWAY

By James Gould Cozzens

*Among modern American writers, James Gould Cozzens appears with increasingly greater stature. "There are a handful like him in every age," said Bernard De Voto. "Later on it turns out that they were the ones who wrote that age's literature."*

*Of* S.S. San Pedro—*a masterpiece of the sea—the* New York Times *wrote: "The . . . author has done more than write a fine story; he has achieved a work of art which is representative of his day, is individual and full of the universal human interest which assures long life to a book."*

*Of* Castaway—*the fantastic story of a man lost in an empty department store—the* Saturday Review *wrote: "Mr. Cozzens is no mean artist in prose, and he has original ideas. He works also with admirable economy of means, and with realistic detail that rivets the attention."*

**MODERN LIBRARY PAPERBACKS** are published by Random House in order to make the best books of all time available to the public at a price it can readily afford.

# S.S. SAN PEDRO

and

# CASTAWAY

JAMES GOULD COZZENS

PUBLISHED BY RANDOM HOUSE
*New York*

*Random House* IS THE PUBLISHER OF *The Modern Library*

BENNETT CERF • DONALD S. KLOPFER • ROBERT K. HAAS

Manufactured in the United States of America

by H. Wolff Book Manufacturing Co.

# CONTENTS

# S.S. SAN PEDRO

*For my Mother*

*in memory of*

*Nova Scotia sea captains*

**1**

June 7, Friday, in the morning, the twin-screw turbine liner *San Pedro,* seventeen thousand tons, lay at her Hoboken pier. To sail at noon on Brixton & Heath's Brazil-River Plate express service, she bore a million dollars in gold for the banking houses of the Argentine. Lashed on her forward well-deck, wedged in number one and number two upper holds, were automobiles, crated, for Montevideo. She carried two thousand tons of cash registers and baking-powder in tins, of cotton shirts and bathtubs, of children's toys, agricultural implements, and a sealed consignment of machine-guns for the government of Paraguay. Coal to bring her out and back loaded her down, overflowing into shelter-deck bunkers forward. Between ten o'clock and half past eleven she took on board one hundred and seventy-two passengers.

Aft, they had a boom out. Trunks were assembled by the half-ton in a corded net on the wharf floor. The boom picked them up easily, swung them into the blaze of the sun. They dropped down number six hatch to the baggage-rooms. Leaning on the rail of the light after-bridge, where he could watch from on high, waited Mr. Bradell, the senior second officer. Mr. Bradell's white-and-gold stood out clean on the heat-dulled blue. A seaman, also white-clad, scarlet semaphore flags thrust under his arm, waited with him, though they would not cast off, Miro knew, for almost an hour.

Miro, first quartermaster, was in direct charge on deck. Miro was Brazilian, coffee-colored from the intense sun and his mixture of bloods, Indian and Negro. Clear and cheerful-eyed, his sound white teeth flashing, his head, erect, covered by a mat of strong black curls which sweat had dampened, he was watching paternally over Packy, the big Jamaican Negro at the winch. Packy was dead drunk, unable to speak, but he remained mechanically precise. He and the winch met at an abysmal level of brainless strength. Like the boom on its gooseneck, Packy pivoted blindly on the small hard point of habit. Like the boom, he described invariably the same controlled semicircles.

Miro stayed behind him in case he should fall unconscious. He was the only person who could manage Packy, and managed by Miro, Packy was perfection. The quartermaster told him so from time to time, in the rich chant of the black lingua franca of the islands. It was equivalent to oil in Packy's bearings and Packy was all right.

Confirming this, Miro shot his eyes up to the white skeleton of the after-bridge, thin on the blue; an eloquent glance to Mr. Bradell, who answered it with a slight mute nod. Miro's whistle shrilled out then, the winch gasped and clanked, the shadow of the boom went swiftly over, the empty net collapsed on the wharf floor. Things were tight, smart, going as they should go.

It was, in Miro's idiom, a matter of *tela*. Integrate with

the Spanish sense of tone, texture, woven firmness was the untranslatable value of a plan, a sustained argument underlying a mode of behavior. It was wide enough to include that beautiful gift of the white man, the disciplined coöperation, speed, and precision of people quick and certain about their duties. This abstraction was the last, perfect pleasure, epitomized by Mr. Bradell in attention alert and quiet above, but, in addition, that a man might know he was good flesh as well as blessed spirit, there were the white uniforms against the sky, the sharp stripe of color in the rolled signal-flags, the smell of hot tar, hot metal, hot salt, of steam and oil and warm wet hemp.

Miro blew on his whistle, jubilant. From his pocket he took out a big gold watch covered with engraved scrolls, a piece of a ruby set on top the stem, fastened to a gold fob, and its magnificence testified to him again the rightness of the world. He worked long and saved, he was quick and quiet, he did not do every foolish thing he thought of, and in the end, with his own money, he could buy such a watch. He looked at it now and noted that it was exactly eleven o'clock. The tugs, he saw, were already off the end of the pier, and with the pleasure of going so soon seaward, he put the watch carefully away, happier if possible than he had been. To Packy he began to sing, throaty and soft, "Hail, Mary, full of grace . . ."

At five minutes past eleven Miro's intelligent eye caught the flicker of the signalman's flags, gay against the serene heavens, answering the navigating bridge. Mr. Bradell turned. He came handily down the ladder, crossing over into the shadows. To Miro he said: "Mr. Fenton will stand by here."

The fourth officer was even then descending from the promenade-deck. Mr. Bradell spoke to him a moment before he mounted quickly out of Miro's sight.

Anthony Bradell, passing the smoking-room doors, avoided the approving glances of two girls. His brown face, at once too thin, too bluntly shaped for any handsomeness, looked none the less like the passenger's idea of a navigating officer. He knew the girls were still watching him as he climbed again to the boat-deck. From the bridge end the quartermaster on duty there hailed him as he came closer. "Captain Clendening in his cabin, Mr. Bradell."

Anthony passed the windows of the wireless-room, saw the first and second operators playing checkers, and raised his hand to the red-headed one. At the passage-door forward he reached in and knocked up the hook which held it ajar. On the captain's door he rapped sharply.

In Captain Clendening's cabin an electric fan vibrated. A tepid shaft of air twitched left to right in a slow arc from the high corner. The captain's radio, muted down, recited intricate directions for some sort of cooking. He must have forgotten to turn it off, not noticing.

Heavy in his white-and-gold, Captain Clendening sat in the swivel chair, back to his desk. He was feeling the terrible waterside heat, Anthony decided, for the captain looked obscurely pale. Wind, tan, years of exposure had given his face a permanent rich color, but this lay now over his cheeks like a surface veneer. Clinging to the sides of his head, his hair, usually a harsh white fur, looked weak and damp. His old blue eyes, always marred by a droop on the left, were unnaturally listless. An early injury to his jaw—Anthony had heard that it was from a thrown marline-spike—made itself felt more and more as the captain grew older, and most today. His right brow arched up round and steep; the left lay flat. The left corner of the mouth sank in a lump outstanding toward the stubborn chin. Over his mouth, strongly set even in this sag, he grew a short mustache, white, like the fur along his head.

He looked at Anthony with an obvious sharp approval.

"Mr. Bradell, our senior second officer," he said, addressing the man on the settee along the wall. "Only sailor on board, God help him. Had his master's papers five years. Just waiting for me to die so the company will have a ship for him." His voice rumbled authentically, but the unwieldy humor was flattened, almost exhausted. It would be impudent, as well as unthinkable, Anthony admitted, to suggest that Mr. Driscoll, the chief officer, be allowed to take the *San Pedro* out. Fortunately ignorant of his thought, Captain Clendening continued: "Bradell, my friend Doctor Percival wants to look the ship over. You can show him about, I guess. Fenton get aft all right?"

"Yes, sir," said Anthony at once. He was blank with astonishment at the inopportunity of the request and he turned sharply toward this man for whom the captain was willing to upset all reasonable routine.

Doctor Percival sat quiet, looking back at Anthony with an accurate, absorbed attention. Doctor Percival's tight face was fleshless and almost gray. His lips sank in, rounded over his teeth. They were lips so scanty that you could see the line of the teeth meeting. His eyes, red-rimmed, lay limp in their sockets, appearing to have no color at all. Doctor Percival's intense pale gaze came out of holes covered with soft, semitransparent lenses. His head, one observed, jolted, was utterly hairless, and a pale-reddish star, a mark like a healed wound, lay across the crown. Every modulation of bone showed through a sere leaf of old skin.

Doctor Percival recognized Anthony's instinctive recoil from this fearful face, and just as obviously prepared to overlook it, indifferent, but he was betrayed by a sudden muscular movement. The whole hollow countenance winced a little; the lips twitched wide in a grimace most like a broken and derisive smile. Anthony stood frozen, for Doctor Percival's eyes denied the expression any significance. It was involuntary; it might, Anthony saw, happen again at any moment. Doctor Percival, with a dignity terrible and silent, held out a gray glove whose palm was dark with moisture. Anthony took it in his own bare brown hand, which he closed hard on the slight, cloth-covered fingers. It was a grip half iron and bone-breaking, but Doctor Percival did not appear to notice. Anthony leveled his gaze out, made his brown eyes look straight into Doctor Percival's colorless ones, and said: "Glad to show you around, Doctor Percival."

He turned at once and opened the door. If he did not feel well, the captain had seen more than enough of that face. Thinking so, Anthony was embarrassed to realize that Doctor Percival somehow understood him, as though he had spoken every word aloud. Doctor Percival was shaking hands with the captain. He said in an exact, highly educated voice: "Take care of yourself until I see you again, John. There is nothing you need to do now." He put his shabby black hat on, stepping out into the passage. Captain Clendening merely nodded. "Good of you to come down, doctor," he said. "Go aft when you finish, Bradell," he added. "Don't like to leave that boy there alone."

Doctor Percival had turned, defeating absolutely Anthony's desire to bring him out on the sunny deck. They went together down the inside stairs at the end. Anthony asked carefully: "What would you like to see, sir?"

He attracted to himself that acute gaze. "I really do not know," Doctor Percival confessed. "It is some time since I have been on a ship—" It was coming, Anthony saw. The broken smile made a kind of irrelevant joke of his last words. Anthony tightened his lips, expressionless.

In the silence ensuing, Doctor Percival, his voice low, said: "But you do not float quite level, do you?"

Astonished, Anthony noticed for the first time that they had, in fact, a slight port list. "We straighten up when we get under weigh," he explained. "We can correct it with the ballast-tanks."

"No danger of tipping over?" asked Doctor Percival.

"Oh, no," said Anthony. "When we're heavily loaded it takes a little adjustment."

"Many passengers?" asked his companion. His voice faded to a husky whisper.

"I don't know exactly," admitted Anthony, resisting the natural temptation to speak low in return. "I should say a hundred and fifty or more."

"And how many men to run the boat?"

"You mean officers?"

"Altogether."

"Oh, we have a crew of two hundred odd."

"Then you carry perhaps four hundred people? It must be a great responsibility?"

Anthony said: "We try to take care of them."

They had been advancing through an alleyway, going aft, which led them out by the purser's office in the main entry. Here it was crowded, confused and noisy.

"The purser's office," Anthony explained needlessly. "The lounge, the public rooms, and so on are above. The dining-room is below there."

Doctor Percival nodded slowly. He looked about him with meticulous attention. He might have been afraid that he was going to overlook something of real importance. "These are passengers, I suppose?" he said.

"Mostly," agreed Anthony.

"Ah," said Doctor Percival. Anthony snapped his eyes

away, detecting the start of that horrid trembling about the mouth. Doctor Percival, he knew now, could not continue speaking until it was past. Anthony had time to notice again the two girls who had admired him aft. One of them was going to smile this time, so he looked back to Doctor Percival. Other people had begun to observe them, considering Doctor Percival's fleshless face and shabby clothes with a sort of electric consternation. Anthony exerted a slight pressure on his companion's arm. "We can go down to the dining-room," he said.

"It would be interesting to see them all eating," Doctor Percival agreed.

"Oh, they're not eating now," answered Anthony. "They don't serve luncheon until after we sail." Anxious to get Doctor Percival out of the lobby, he had been prepared to assist him downstairs. The firmness of the man's step abashed him. Doctor Percival, Anthony realized, was not exactly old. He was simply not young. And far from being weak, he had an unexpected inert strength. His steps fell heavy as stones, despite his slight appearance.

"This is the dining-room," said Anthony.

"Ah," said Doctor Percival, "that is interesting. Would it be possible to see the machinery?"

Anthony hesitated at the dining-room doors. Here the chief steward was assigning tables to a line of people waiting, and all these seemed to turn at once, attracted by those steps on the stairs. They gaped at Doctor Percival. "Yes," said Anthony, deciding to risk Mr. MacGillivray's annoyance, if only he could get his companion out of the way somewhere. "We could stop in a moment. We could look at the engines from above. They're pretty busy now, of course."

They went down the alleyway. "We just step in here,"

Anthony said. "I'm afraid you'll be pretty warm, sir. Would you like to take your overcoat off?"

"No, no," said Doctor Percival. "I don't feel heat."

Anthony twisted the iron handle. Up to them almost overwhelming, came the hot oily breath, the surge of sound in the engine-room shaft. Anthony closed the door and they stood together on the landing outside the chief engineer's office. Anthony glanced in fleetingly, saw Mr. MacGillivray sitting at his desk, the shirt on his back soaked with patches of sweat, his sleeves rolled up on his big freckled arms. He was busy with some papers.

Doctor Percival put his gloved hands on the rail.

"That's dirty, I'm afraid, sir," warned Anthony, raising his voice. "There really isn't much to see. They're warming up the turbines now. Those are the turbines there, those big green things."

"Ah," nodded Doctor Percival. Anthony's face hardened, but he held his eyes unwavering. "They supply the power, I presume," Doctor Percival said when it was over. His harsh whisper was entirely clear, neither lower nor louder than it had seemed outside.

"Of course, there's an astern turbine, too," Anthony shouted. "Not much to see—"

The chief was coming out of his office. He paused, surprised, and stared at Anthony coldly. "Just showing a friend of the captain's what we've got," Anthony said. "Doctor Percival, this is Mr. MacGillivray, the chief engineer."

Mr. MacGillivray gave him one steady look. He put out a hand with enlarged knuckles covered by loose freckled skin and hosts of pale hairs. He closed it like a trap on Doctor Percival's glove. "Sorry I haven't more time," he said briefly. Disturbing his resemblance to a mild and friendly bloodhound, his face began to harden. It hung free from the cheek-bones, but stiffly now. In the folds, stubbled with two days' blond beard, his mouth was usually lost. Now his lips pouted out solidly. Pale china blue, his eyes peered with a candid dislike beneath his big brows. Even the skin of his forehead, white from three decades under electric lights, colored a little in gathering irritation.

Doctor Percival ignored this change. "Are they very powerful?" he inquired huskily. He made a fragmentary gesture toward the turbine cases.

After a while Mr. MacGillivray roared: "Oh, we get twelve thousand shaft horse-power." He started brusquely to go down the steps. Then he halted. He made it plain that he considered this visitor an emergency requiring his presence. He waited while Doctor Percival neither said anything nor moved. Finally Mr. MacGillivray raised a hand and shouted: "Mr. Forsay! Ask can we try!"

Below, a head in a dirty white cap which had been studying the micrometers tilted up a face and yelled back: "Ask to try, sir." It turned then and bent over the desk toward the bridge telephone.

"What is it you are going to do now?" Doctor Percival asked.

"See if we work," said the chief bluntly.

"Try away, sir!" sang up the voice.

"Port engine, Mr. Forsay!"

"Port engine, sir."

"They always do work, I suppose," observed Doctor Percival. He removed his hat and Mr. MacGillivray almost stepped back, seeing the hairless skull and the jagged reddish star. "Never know till they do," he said, swallowing.

The three of them stood there, staring down in silence, as though they awaited a sign or a miracle. A bell clashed out; simultaneously signal-lights winked red. At once, like the first man breathed on by God, the *San Pedro* was com-

ing alive. From her own boilers the unspeakable breath
of superheated steam inspired her. Strong as ten thousand
horses it broke out in the steel vitals of the port turbine.
With stunning impact, it ricocheted, smashing off the sta-
tionary vanes. It impinged like a hundred sledge-hammers
on the converse rotor blades. Now, you might think, the
*San Pedro* contracted its mighty muscles and girded its
loins. The shaft-barrel, locked in the ponderous triple grip
of the balancing pistons, steadied to a frustrated quiver.
It strained titanically. It yielded. Twisting their film of oil
to a lather, the journal-bearings revolved. The great thrust-
bearing braced in obdurate mastery. Far astern, dim in
the water beyond the hull, over went the big blades of the
port-propeller. The *San Pedro* winced ahead in her moor-
ings.

Mr. MacGillivray turned his eyes coldly on Doctor Percival. "They work," he snapped, and while he spoke Doctor Percival's face twitched, the mouth broke to pieces.
Mr. MacGillivray stared at him.

"Port engine okay, sir," shouted up Mr. Forsay.

"You a passenger?" asked Mr. MacGillivray, paying no
attention.

"No," said Doctor Percival. He opened the door himself
and stepped into the alleyway.

"Listen!" Mr. MacGillivray roared to Anthony. "Don't
you know any better than to bring these dumb-bells in when
we're warming up, son? Down here, we work. And furthermore, I don't like your friend. Now, get out!"

Anthony stepped, flushed and warm, into the alleyway
too. He closed the door. Doctor Percival was looking at him
with absorbed colorless attention, and Anthony said, flus-
tered: "The chief's pretty sharp-tongued. He doesn't mean
anything, though."

Doctor Percival whispered: "I do not blame him. He

has a great responsibility, after all, keeping those engines. You would be entirely helpless without them, wouldn't you?"

"We'd be in a bad way," Anthony admitted. "Did you say you wanted to go ashore, sir?"


They came up the stairs by the dining-room and through the press of the main entry. The third officer was at the head of the gangway. He looked at Anthony and then at his companion and whistled soundlessly. "Ready to put off, Mr. Bradell," he said.

"Yes, I must go," said Doctor Percival. A light somewhat more distinct came into the pale holes of his lensed eyes. "The captain," he said very low to Anthony, "is an old man, Mr. Bradell."

"What did you say, sir?" asked Anthony, taken aback.

"People grow old, Mr. Bradell. They break down, they wear out."

"If you consider him worn out, sir," said Anthony sharply, "you're wrong. You can ask the ship's doctor about that."

"I have no interest in the opinion of ship's doctors," whispered Doctor Percival. He closed his eyes a moment. "I am merely mentioning a fact."

"It isn't my place to discuss anything like that with you, sir," said Anthony.

"This is not a discussion, Mr. Bradell," said Doctor Percival.

"I am afraid I must go," said Anthony.

"Yes," said Doctor Percival, unannoyed, "you must. So must I."

"Second gong's gone, Mr. Bradell," called the third officer, impatient.

Doctor Percival made no effort either to thank him or
to shake hands. He had not halted a moment while he was
speaking. Now his unhurried progress simply bore him on,
leaving Anthony behind. The sun, slanting almost perpendicular between the edge of the wharf roof and the *San
Pedro's* side, lay hot on the slope of the gangplank. Doctor
Percival's black figure moved there, passed on; was lost
in deep shadows ashore.

The third officer whistled again, audibly this time. Anthony turned aft to take over Mr. Fenton's charge.

In the sun of the deck below he passed Miro and the carpenter's mate busy with the hatch covers. At the top of the
ladder Mr. Fenton touched his cap smartly. The semaphore flags awoke on the navigating bridge. "We'll cast
off," nodded Anthony. Mr. Fenton said: "We've got quite
a list, haven't we?"

"Straighten it up under weigh—" Anthony started to
say, but the great rising roar of the *San Pedro's* whistle
drowned him out.

**2**

Steady and strong through the infinite ocean twilight the
*San Pedro* maintained her seventeen knots. The vital
quiver of her engines gave her a mounting wave of vibra-

tion, like a piano feeling the pedal. Her warm untroubled breath trembled up her shafts and ventilators. She was calm in the lucid radiance of her early lights. Around the dining-room a whole half-deck of her stirred with more intense activity. In the balcony the orchestra was gathering; by the buffet the chief steward was checking the flowers on the many tables. He made a sign to his assistant that the doors might be opened when he heard the gong. Aft, the smoking-room was murmuring, expansive in crowded comfort; ice rattled in the bright bar; mild air moved in the doors open on the deck behind. Seen from here, the smoke-soiled mast with the hidden glow of the running light, the booms laid down, the dim sunset radiance remaining on the steerage superstructure, all rose and fell together gently. Astern, the quiet ocean, neither blue nor black, extended in limitless ease to the faintly colored horizon, darkening now to evening at the end of the *San Pedro's* steady white wake.

On the navigating bridge, Mr. Eberly, the junior second officer, had the watch. A helmsman was planted at the wheel. A quartermaster with folded arms stared away into the dusk beside him. In the chart-room behind, Captain Clendening wrote the night orders under the glow of a green-shaded lamp. Calculations from the wireless-room informed him of the vessels to be met or overtaken before morning, and the approximate times they would come abreast. He noted them down one after another as a caution to the watch-officer. Many of these ships he knew; on two of them the masters were old acquaintances. Thinking about these friends, he wrote more slowly. The overwhelming monotony and weariness of the sea weighed him down. Bound north, bound south, the same ships, the

same men were always passing. On his own ship, when
he went to dinner, passengers impossible to distinguish
from a thousand others, doubly regimented by what the
company considered importance, would be at his table—
all the same; only their names were different. In many
cases even the names might be the same and he must recall previous voyages, details of personality and business.
He pressed the buzzer. The quartermaster came, took the
sheet and posted it on the bridge board. Muffled, the metallic throb of the hammered dinner-gong rose, but Captain
Clendening remained motionless, wondering how many
more voyages he would be good for, and what would be
left then but death, so slow, so horribly swift.

Below, on the engine-room shaft, Mr. MacGillivray sat
in his office. He was vigorously scrubbed and shaved. His
uniform coat was buttoned neatly over his round belly. He
wore a low stiff collar and a black silk tie. While he glanced
at the afternoon reports he cleaned his fingernails, digging
slowly and methodically with a pocket-file. Placid, clean,
and comfortable, he was pleased at the thought of a table-
ful of new people who would presently await him in the
dining-room. He took time to rehearse one or two of the
suitable anecdotes which had served him well on twenty
trips. All the while up to him poured the fine steam and
steel symphony of full-ahead. His big ears, with the pale
blond hairs growing out of them, cocked to it invisibly, he
was exhilarated by the perfect correctness of its blended
noises. In his mind's eye this peace of good performance
took the envisioned shape of the long submarine shaft al-
leys, their spaced electric lights winking on the great shafts
revolving. Liquid with oil, brighter than silver, they spun
serenely on their bearings, ninety times a minute.

The dinner-gong aroused him and he arose contentedly,
giving his nails one last critical inspection. He stopped and

waved his hand to the watch-officer below to show that he was leaving. Then he pulled in his stomach as far as it would go, straightened his shoulders. His face began to beam with urbane anticipation: and out he went, sedately.

In the fire-room, like almost heroic figures against the hell of the swung-open doors, the black gang stood to its furnaces. Wheelbarrows from the bunker chutes rattled on the steel flooring. Covers rang successively shut. The chief fireman swigged down a half-pint of tepid tea, retaining some of it to spit sizzling on the hot iron. Swinging his gorilla arms, rolling up his eyes, the crazy man called Quail balanced on his shovel handle and began to intone hoarse organ notes which suddenly merged into the "St. Louis Blues." The Haitian Negroes simply stared at him, but those from the Barbados and Jamaica had picked up the words and felt the long sad pull of the music. They wiped their foreheads and raised their voices. The chief fireman said: "Never mind that, Bo! All you got to do is work." But there was no sense in trying to tell Quail anything. The only things he could understand, he knew already—food, liquor, and shoveling. Just under the roar of the fans, the forced drafts, and the clamor of the moving machinery their chant rose in a musical thick moan, a muffled lament fading between the great overjutting boilers. The chief fireman, his eyes sternly on the dials, gave way after a moment and moaned with them.

In his cabin Anthony Bradell was shaving. His face was half covered with lather and he held his razor motionless from time to time, listening to Miro, who stood stiffly in the corner at a sort of attention. Miro continued: "Six four are twenty-four; six five are thirty; six six are forty-two—"

"Try again," grunted Anthony.

"Thirty-six, sir," responded Miro, inspired. He had been many months on the multiplication tables, for he could see no reason to hurry. Mr. Bradell thought a quartermaster ought to be working for a third mate's license, but Miro knew it would be useless to him, since he meant to remain in Brixton & Heath's employ as long as Mr. Bradell was on a Brixton & Heath ship. The company could never advance any one with Negro blood. Miro understood this perfectly and it did not trouble him, for he had no desire to be advanced. Life gave him now everything he wanted and penalized him not at all. He even enjoyed trying to learn mathematics, not through any desire to determine latitude by meridian altitude, but because such activity was *tela;* something stern and difficult to be done, unspoiled by any completion or end in view. In time, if Mr. Bradell's patience should seem to wear thin, he would make no effort for Mr. Bradell's sake and submit to examinations. He was not alarmed at the possibility of passing. Mr. Bradell would not want him to stop there. The requirements for a second mate's papers might legitimately be made into the work of centuries. Miro could, he was calmly sure, never learn anything about longitude by chronometer. Deviation of the compass by an amplitude or an azimuth would be certainly impossible. He must be old, probably dead, before he satisfied Mr. Bradell about them. Concluding his recitation he smiled eloquently and said: "I will study them again, sir."

"It will come easier," promised Anthony, who thought he might be discouraged. "Better turn in now. You've had a hard day."

"Good night, sir," agreed Miro. He was happy to have made so little progress. "Thank you very much, sir."

There was starlight on the forward deck. Here Miro leaned a moment on the rail, feeling the moist wind in his face, watching the soft sea break open about the *San Pedro's* advancing stem, filming up her prow and falling off. She was constructed with very little freeboard, so the water was close and fast. He noticed that she still listed slightly. This displeased him. As they said in the islands, where they had picked it up from the Royal Navy, it was not "tiddly."

He entered the door at last and went to find Packy. As he expected, Packy was half off his bunk. With a tolerant shove of his foot he pushed Packy securely against the wall, for he expected it to blow up before morning. Then he bent down and searched underneath until he found the corked gin bottle. This he took, to lock in his own box, so the boatswain would not find it and throw it overboard. Packy would need miserably one stiff drink some time during the forenoon. In a position to bargain with him, Miro could force Packy to assign him all his money. Then Packy, ashore in the South, could not get mixed up with some woman who might make him miss the boat.

In the quartermaster's bunk-room Miro stripped to his underwear, wrapped himself in a blanket, and lay staring up in the dim light. Contented, he recommended himself to the Cuban Virgin of Cobre, to San Juan de Matha, and to San Pedro Tomás, all of whom had kindly superintended men at sea.

Left alone, Anthony Bradell finished his shaving. A fresh uniform lay on his bunk and he considered it without pleasure while he put away his shaving things, restoring his cabin to its brutally bare and immaculate good order. It was an idea of the company that some officers not on duty should go down after dinner when the passengers were dancing in the widened waist of the promenade-deck and make themselves agreeable. On most of the company's vessels leadership in this fell conveniently to the chief officer, who stood no watch. Mr. Driscoll of the *San Pedro* was not a success socially. Captain Clendening had selected Anthony instead. He did not, he told his senior second officer when he gave the order, know what the hell the sea had come to, but the *San Pedro* might as well make as good a showing as possible. Anthony could leave at ten o'clock, and he needn't come onto the morning watch until four bells on such nights. Mr. Fenton, who acted as his junior watch-officer, was perfectly competent. Anthony agreed about the fourth officer's competence. He did not consider sleep precisely a vice, but any concern about it failed to fit in with the efficient asceticism he had brought himself to practice. He would continue to be called as usual.

The captain, perfectly aware of this, added in a better temper that Anthony would report to the captain's cabin at ten. "First thing you know," he explained with a grimly bawdy sardonicism, "you'll be up on the boat-deck with some little piece in skirts."

It was his method of chiding an exaggerated stiffness in Anthony's attitude. He drove the point home by pulling down from the small row of books the Revised Statutes. He bent the volume open to Section 280 and asked him ironically to consider the fate of the erring officer ". . . who 'during the voyage under promise of marriage, or by threats, or the exercise of authority, or solicitation—' that includes standing around in uniform, boy," he interpolated, "—'or the making of gifts or presents, seduces and has illicit connection with any female passenger, shall be fined not more than one thousand dollars or imprisoned for not more than one year. . . .' Or both," he added. "Hardly ever worth it."

Anthony agreed, with composure. Like himself, the captain was an inarticulate man. On the rare occasions when he chose to soften his formal attitude he could resort only to this gruff and tortuous humor. It expressed for him a paternal affection, of which his long training at sea made him instinctively avoid any show. Anthony, who was more attached to him and respected him more than any other human being, understood. Captain Clendening, knowing he did, put the relationship away with the book, snapped closed and returned to the shelf. "That's all, Mr. Bradell," he said. "I'll expect you to stand by below on quiet evenings."

Anthony said: "Yes, sir."

He had been doing it for over a year now. By degrees this customary thoroughness made him an adequate dancer, but it was purely a matter of discipline. The fact remained that it was a silly thing for a seaman to be doing.

Tonight he considered with positive apprehension those two girls who had first seen him aft and then again with Doctor Percival in the entry. They would be enthusiastic dancers. He could only hope that during the afternoon they might have attached some desirable males who would monopolize them.

The watch had changed and Mr. Eberly, coming belatedly to his quarters, stuck in his round face and said: "Going to knock them dead, Bradell?"

This was perhaps the two hundred and fiftieth repetition of that question, so Anthony didn't think it needed an answer. Mr. Eberly usually came down himself and liked it, so Anthony said: "You'd better get going. You might miss some of it. Couple of kids I'm going to see you meet."

"Thanks," said Mr. Eberly. "Dumb-looking lot of women on this trip."

Dimly from the lower deck dance-music beat up now and Mr. Eberly withdrew. Anthony, severe and noncommittal, went out. At the wireless-room he paused. "What do you get?" he asked, standing into the light of the door.

Morris, the second operator, was on duty. A cigarette sagged out of the corner of his mouth. One of his head-phones was pushed up, resting against his reddish hair. The other dug tight into his left ear. His pointed young face turned, flippant in profile, suiting itself to the un-original jargon of his ready mockery. He spoke at once, with the accent, jeering, tight-voweled, of poor Boston streets. "Plenty," he said. "Bad weather south. Force seven and getting worse. We'll catch it, I guess. Had the *San Pablo* for a few minutes. The old man wanted to know where they were. Finally got a QRN off them. You'd think they were in China. Tell your girl friends they'll all be sick tomorrow."

"Right with me," said Anthony. "Hurry it up if you can."

"You're just a minor error," sighed Morris. "I wish I could see some women without a grill to protect them."

Anthony moved down the deck. The *San Pedro's* funnel was steaming against the stars. He felt the warm blast of the engine-room shaft, and then the mild ocean air, as he turned in the stairs. Japanese lanterns had been strung along the deck. He advanced into this dusk, standing near the orchestra in the corner. The two girls, who had gotten into elaborate dinner-dresses, noticed him at once, but the press of people dancing interfered with their advance. They managed it gradually, around the edges, arm in arm, until they stood beside him with an appearance of accident so preposterous that Anthony groaned inwardly and gave way. "Nice evening, isn't it?" he said.

"Do you run this ship?" inquired the blond one engagingly. "Because, if you do, I wish you'd fix it."

"It's completely cock-eyed," her companion informed him, more calmly. "It doesn't sit straight. You don't notice it much until you try to dance. Then you just slide over to the rail."

Her eyebrows rose, miraculously slim and black. She used a heavy warm scent, some modification of the patchouli Anthony associated with the segregated districts of the Southern ports. She ought to be spanked, he decided, but he said in the manner he had developed for passengers: "I'll speak to the captain about it. I wouldn't be surprised if he had it fixed by morning."

He could dance with her, if he liked, she announced negligently. "Clara won't mind. There comes her brother. If I only knew your name I could introduce him to you, couldn't I?"

Anthony met a frail, blond young man with a minimum of mild chin. Mr. Mills. The girl called Clara took her brother's arm and said: "Come back to the smoking-room when you finish and have a drink. That means you, Mr. Bradell."

"I'd be delighted to come back," Anthony said stiffly, "but I'm afraid it isn't customary for us to drink."

"The custom should be changed," said the dark girl. "But you do dance?

"You don't know my name," she added, fitting herself to him with graceful completeness and precision. "It's Marilee." It would be, Anthony decided, morose. "You have only one name, I suppose," she went on.

The wan warm scent of the brothels of Rio enveloped

him. "What would I do with an extra one?" he asked.

Her hair came against his gold epaulet, her lips parted slightly. "Does your sweetheart call you Bradell?" she inquired. "This music isn't bad, considering what makes it. You'd have quite a nice little boat here if you could only get it to stand straight."

"It takes you there and back," answered Anthony.

"You dance divinely, don't you?" she said. "If we only had decent music and a decent floor you'd be marvelous. Am I going to like Buenos Aires?"

"No way of knowing," said Anthony.

"You mean you don't know what I like. That's odd. I feel as though I knew all about you—er—Bradell."

This was more than his painfully developed passenger manner could handle, Anthony admitted, provoked. As to what she liked, if her dancing were any indication, that wouldn't be hard. His mind supplied it, curt, unprintable. He remembered, not without a pleasure in its rigidity, his duty to the passengers. For seeing that this Marilee creature enjoyed her trip so much that Brixton & Heath's competitors didn't get her return passage, he supposed grimly that he was responsible.

In his customary pride of self-control he said: "The name is Anthony."

"Too late," she answered. "I like Bradell better. There! There isn't any more. Thanks loads, Bradell. Let's get a drink."

She detached herself from him with a soft reluctance, sliding an arm through his and turning him aft. "Every one will think I've made a conquest," she said. "Only you and I know how false it is."

At least, Anthony realized, he was being spared perhaps the worst feature of this business, which was having to say something. She was apparently considering his silence, for she asked now: "Have you really a sweetheart somewhere you're afraid you won't be true to? Or do you just hate women? Or are you queer?"

"Just queer," said Anthony briefly.

Her laughter spilled around the corner. "Bradell," she said, "I don't believe it."

"Don't believe what?" he asked, embarrassed.

"Queer." She laughed again.

Anthony went scarlet. "You're pretty loose with your language, aren't you?" he said impotently.

"Awful," she agreed. "I have to be to make any impression on you, Bradell. How can I help where I lose my heart?" She brought him into the smoking-room, up to a table where the blond girl and Mr. Mills sat drinking. "I expect I'd better get back," Anthony said.

"Sit down, Bradell," said Marilee, "or I'll scream."

She easily might, Anthony decided. On the whole it would be simpler to sit down. She ordered a stinger. "A split of vichy," Anthony answered Mr. Mills's question.

"I'm glad to see there's no drunkenness among the ship's officers," Marilee sighed, leaning forward on her elbows. "You aren't drunk, are you, Bradell?"

Miss Mills seemed to think this was funny, but her brother looked thoroughly disapproving. Anthony was astonished to find how disreputable Mr. Mills's absence of chin made disapproval. He couldn't share it as heartily as he wished. "Only speak lower," he requested. "Tomorrow the captain will be asking me whether there's so much smoke with no fire."

She, personally, said Marilee, would reassure the captain. Nothing she had ever seen was so proper as Bradell. "By the way," she went on, frowning, "who was that—er—old gentleman in black I saw you with?"

"A friend of the captain's," Anthony answered, startled.

"He's not on board, is he?"

"No. He went ashore."

"That's fine," she nodded. "I thought I saw him tonight. He gave me the willies. I'm not fooling you, Bradell.
I darn near marched ashore. I'll bet I'll see him in my
dreams. You don't suppose he was dead, do you?"

"Certainly not," said Anthony, staggered. "His name's
Doctor Percival. He—"

"Never mind. I don't want to hear any more," she said
sharply. "He ought to be buried. He hasn't any business
scaring me to death. Bradell, I don't like to meet corpses
walking around. It means something awful is going to happen to me."

"Don't be silly," said Anthony with unconscious di-
rectness. "I understood he wasn't well. That's why he
looked—"

"Keep still, Bradell," she begged, "I know all about
that. One more dance and I'll let you go—for tonight. . . ."

He arose and she came and took his arm. Outside she
drew him a minute to the rail, gazing down at the lights on
the flying water, the dim white crests of the outrushing hull
wave. "Looks cool," she remarked.

"Keep out of it," said Anthony. "It costs us a lot of
money to stop."

"I'll keep out," she agreed. "God, Bradell, I'd hate to
drown. No fooling."

Anthony approached the wireless-room again. Couch, the
night operator, was just relieving Morris. Morris stepped
out on deck. "Hi, Bradell," he said. "Look where you're
taking us."

They both glanced up at the thickening sky, starless now. Underfoot, the *San Pedro* was beginning to feel the sea. Her smooth fore-and-aft motion swung off-center deliberately, beginning a roll. From the starboard bow an occasional faint crash of jostled water reached them.

"Better put the cork in," said Morris. "They're going to shake us well before using."

"Maybe not," said Anthony. "We're headed pretty well out. Taken your Mother Sill's?"

"And expected to live," nodded Morris. "Hold on a minute. Going to see the old man? I got the *San Pablo* again. Maybe he'd like to hear they have nothing to report. Couch," he called, "let's have that last bridge report." He reached through the window. "There you are," he said. "Get it to Garcia."

Anthony went forward. The wind, coming up, made the passage-door hard to open. Inside he paused at the captain's cabin.

"Bradell turning in, sir," he called. "Memorandum on the *San Pablo* under the door. Okay, sir?"

"Step in," came Captain Clendening's voice.

Anthony pushed the door open. The captain was lying on his berth, a magazine in his hands, the reading-light in the corner on. A half-consumed cigar was locked in his teeth. He had got into pajamas and a brilliant silk dressing-gown. Above and behind him, the light cast deep shadows over his eyes. He had his radio on, very quiet, and a low throb of dance-music from New York filled the cigar-hazed air. "Where's the *San Pablo?*" he asked. Anthony handed him the slip. "They ought to be farther along," the captain said fretfully.

"Want them for something, sir?"

"No, no." Captain Clendening threw the magazine aside. "What good are they?"

The cigar had gone out. "Light, sir?" said Anthony, picking up a match-box.

"Never mind, boy," said Captain Clendening.

"Smoke too much. Something wrong with my guts."

"Suppose I fix you some bicarb, sir?"

"No good." Captain Clendening ran a hand irritably through the white fur above his ear. "I've got to take care of myself, I guess." He was silent a moment. From New York the foxtrot beat on, smooth and sweet. "Nice music," he said, noticing it. "How's it out?"

"Blowing up, sir."

"I felt it," he nodded. "Where do you suppose we get this list from? Ring up the engine-room and see if we're making any."

Astonished, Anthony took the engine-room telephone.

"Captain wants your bilge soundings," he said. "Ring back. We've got a good load, sir," he continued.

"I guess so," said the captain. "Saw we were wetting our marks."

"Not much, sir," protested Anthony, astonished again. "Nothing much. That's the wharfinger's fault. He—"

"Don't you believe that, boy!" roared Captain Clendening. "Don't let me hear you say things like that. You're a sailor, not a steward."

Anthony colored a little. "I meant," he ventured, "we seem to have to take what we can get, sir."

Captain Clendening jerked his head, twitching his mustache. "Don't feel well," he said more mildly. "You mustn't pay any attention to it. Felt like snapping some one's head off, and you were here, that's all. Great thing to have your youth, boy. You can't keep it, but you ought to think about it sometimes. No point in sleeping through."

The telephone buzzed. Anthony took it up. Turning from it, he said: "They're dry, sir."

"Well, tell them to pump out number two port ballast-tank before morning. Got to straighten us up. God knows what could happen, running into a gale this way."

Anthony returned to the telephone. He must have shown his amazement at concern so exaggerated, for the captain's low left eye winked with a sort of embarrassment. The sagging lump on that side of his chin stood out more. He grunted: "When your insides go back on you it shakes you all up. Just little things. They all get together and you—all of a sudden you see you aren't going to live forever. I'm damned if I know why any one at sea today wants to live at all, but you do, you do." He bit the dead cigar, the stiff bristles of his mustache brushing it. "You don't like going out, boy. Sort of cold. Sort of lonely. Well, we all got to do it."

The bare blaze of light in the corner, the smoke-filmed air, the harsh photographs of ships—former commands of Captain Clendening's, some lost in the war, some broken up—and especially the captain himself, his hard face puffy in a relaxed brooding, his lumpy form bent a little under the gay silk of the dressing-gown, repeated louder than his words: cold, lonely, old. "They break down," Anthony remembered, "they wear out."

Now, at this bleak moment, the dim contented blare of dance-music fluctuated, feeling the stronger atmospherics. It sagged like a long thread, dipped down, and the mighty ocean covered it in silence. It drew taut again, came fleetingly into earshot, and then it parted. The *San Pedro* drew away in the immense abyss of winds, in the caverns of black water. Only, the *San Pedro* was built for stress; the great turbines turning could never grow tired; the renewed watch above was always sleepless. Men, it seemed to Anthony, were not so well made for living. Energy, power, the vital confidence, grew low as the void grew larger, the ocean mightier and more immense. Eyes wore out with watching; they neither saw nor cared finally—

The *San Pedro* lurched, put her prow hard into rising water, shook from stem to stern. Spray fanned up, curved with the wind and fell in a rippling tap on the starboard ports.

"Took a deep one," said Anthony, rousing himself.

"Turn in, boy," said the captain. "We'll have a wet night."

"Suppose I make a turn around and see that all's secure."

"No. Driscoll did it. Get sleep, boy. Turn in. Forget about it all. May run out by morning."

"Why don't I ask the doctor to step up a minute, sir? He could give you something for your stomach and you'd get a good rest."

"You saw my doctor here this morning," said Captain Clendening. "He knows all about me. He said I ought to be careful. But there wasn't anything to do. I expect I'll rest all right, boy, I'll rest."

**3**

Miro had to drop his oilskins. He caught the hand-rail on the wall, extended his other hand and found Mr. Bradell's shoulder. He shook hard. "One bell, sir," he announced.

"Thick weather. Gale from south. Sea high. Temperature, forty-seven."

Anthony sat up at once, swung his legs out and rubbed his eyes.

"Wet on the bridge, sir," said Miro. He held onto the rail. "Let's have a light," Anthony said.

The *San Pedro* with a sort of wanton fury must have shouldered a hill of water off her bows. She shuddered distractedly, she seemed to jump up and down. A hundred sharp sounds of her rebelling frame rose in chorus. Like resolutely planted kicks the throb of her engines hit her behind. Caught thus between two hardly resistible forces, the *San Pedro* staggered sideways, the floor tilted, the wall receded. There was a vindictive crash of water, a sort of double jolt as her screws approached the surface.

"Plenty rough," yawned Anthony. He threw a towel into the basin, held on tight and let the water soak it, flung it, one-handed, over his face and head, mopping.

"I got your coffee in a bottle, sir," said Miro.

"Pull out my old uniform, if you can," requested Anthony. Water shook from his hair and his face shone. He took the bottle. The coffee he gulped in precarious scalding swallows and it flooded his stomach with a fine hot exhilaration. Bracing himself on the bunk edge, he dressed, putting a sweater on under his uniform coat. "Been like this long?" he asked.

"Not so bad," answered Miro. "It got worse, ten-twenty minutes ago. We don't come back very well. Glass gone on the port promenade, a steward told me."

Anthony stamped into his boots, jerked the leather strap at the collar of his slicker and pulled the waterproof hood over his uniform cap. Above, in the warm chartroom, he paused and initialed the night orders. "No change in course," he said.

"It does not seem so, sir," said Miro. He caught Anthony's arm in one hand and the table edge in the other.

"Thanks," nodded Anthony. They came out.

Mr. Fenton wasn't up yet, but the helmsman had been relieved. Mr. Sheedy, the extra second officer on the midwatch, grunted with obvious gratitude. "This course is south," he said formally, "fourteen degrees east."

"South fourteen degrees east," Anthony echoed. He stepped deftly against the roll and came next to the engine-room telegraph.

"Say, this a rotten blow," announced Sheedy. "We're listing plenty. Do you notice?"

"Partly the wind," said Anthony.

"And partly wet water. Why don't you ring up the old man and ask him to let you point off a bit? We get it square in the eye."

"Blow over in a minute, perhaps."

"Carpenter's having a bad time with the port half-door. Can't get it secure, poor devil. Driscoll's up too, or at least he was, but he didn't call the old man. I hear we broke some glass just now."

Fenton came out, wincing. "God, I cracked my elbow a hot one," he said, stung out of the formalities of bridge etiquette. "What is this, a circus?"

"So long," said Sheedy.

Fenton touched his hidden cap brim.

"I'll step out, Mr. Fenton," Anthony said. "Quartermaster, take a look around starboard." He made his way to the door and let himself onto the open bridge gingerly, moving down the rail almost hand over hand to the shelter at the end. Breathing hard and dripping, he looked forward and the dim radiance of the running light, the glow from the bridge, showed him they were taking it white over the bows every other minute. Fine for those automobiles, he thought. I hope they packed them dry. Growing accustomed to the darkness, he could make out the deck below, and judged that no lines were rigged. It made him wonder what Mr. Driscoll could be doing. He turned and stared aft, but he couldn't see beyond the dim shape of the first life-boat. Something must have happened to the light over the stairs. Bending a little he pulled himself back to the door. Inside he drew off his dripping gloves and went to the telephone.

The minute's long silence broke in his ear with a clean click. "Navigating bridge, sir," he said. "Bradell speaking."

"Well, boy?" came Captain Clendening's voice.

"Permission to change course, sir? Pretty wet forward."

"Do what you want. Shall I come up?"

"No, sir. Nothing wrong."

"Half-speed, Mr. Fenton," Anthony requested. "Half-speed, sir," agreed Mr. Fenton, snapping over the telegraph.

"Helm!" said Anthony. The helmsman glanced over his shoulder, stood aside, fastening both hands on one spoke. Anthony stepped in and took it. He drew the wheel right, hand over hand. The electric telltale went to half rudder.

"Port full ahead, Mr. Fenton!"

"Port full ahead, sir."

The *San Pedro* gained steerageway, came staggering over. She buried her starboard bow and the white water thundered down. She tilted up and rode the next one. "Two-thirds, Mr. Fenton."

The telltale went amidships. Anthony bent his face into the binnacle light. "The course is due south," he said. "Look alive! Nothing off."

The helmsman stood on.

"Well," sighed Mr. Fenton, "I guess the worst is over."

At six o'clock, dawn, delayed, was pale on the forecastle.
Miro relieved the helmsman. Anthony had attempted full
ahead twice, but they made wet work of it. Captain Clendening, up to the ears in his bridge coat, appeared now.
He returned the salute of the watch incompletely, holding
onto a window and staring out forward. He stood so long,
swaying loosely with the movement of the ship, that even
Miro at the helm began to watch him, apprehensive.

"What are we doing, Mr. Bradell?" he said at last.
"About two knots?"

"About five, sir, I think."

"List is worse," he said. He came and stared at the
clinometer. "Anything shifted yet?"

"Not that I know of, sir."

"Where's Mr. Driscoll?"

"I think he's still below, sir, at the half-door. They were
making quite a lot of water."

"I want to see him. Look up the chief officer, Mr. Fenton."

His face in the strengthening light was so haggard that
Anthony said: "Take some coffee, sir. The vacuum bottle's full in the chart-room."

"Don't want it now," he answered. "Turn out the morning watch, Mr. Bradell. I want to heave to and find out
what's wrong with us. What do we need for steerageway?"

"I guess one-third, sir."

"All right. Helm! Mind your rudder. Get on, Mr. Bradell."


Anthony supposed it was ten o'clock when the fore-and-aft
bulkhead in upper hold number one stove. Two cased automobiles shifted fifteen feet to port, knocking down the wall

of the port bunk-room. The wedges probably came loose when they had lain-to while wind and sea on their port quarter shook them so heavily. That helpless half-hour had been a little worse than futile, then. He went forward with Mr. Eberly. The junior second officer said: "Well, maybe the old man will feel better now. We got something wrong here all right."

Anthony understood Mr. Eberly's attitude but he understood too Captain Clendening's earlier exasperation at their failure to find anything which would account for the list. He said nothing now, viewing the bunk-room attentively. In the working alleyway there was water over his ankles. At the half-door Mr. Driscoll was still busy in a grim, conscientious silence. He had several seamen with him and they were trying to tighten the dogs with a persistence which had become, considering the simplicity of the task, merely maddening. Anthony had an impatient desire to get at that job himself and finish it up. It was too senseless. They had been working there off and on for eight hours without effecting a change. To avoid any such officiousness he turned back to Mr. Eberly and said: "We'd gone over pretty far to make them slide. This sea will have to go down before we can do much. I don't believe they'll move again."

"Say, listen, white man," rose a querulous voice from the firemen's forecastle beyond, "how we sleep?"

"Pipe down!" called Anthony sharply.

"We got water, mister."

He went up the passage. "Oh," he said, "you have a port out."

The bunk-room was running underfoot. Two electric bulbs burned and sickly morning light came with the recurring splashes of water through the broken port. A strong smell arose; wet wool and bedding, old sweat.

Wrapped in blankets, like lively mummies on shelves, forms stirred, white eyeballs rolled in the shadows. The crazy man, Quail, caught the iron bunk post above, swung himself out and down with one arm, like a chimpanzee. He landed squatly on his feet in the shallow water. "I want to be home," he moaned. He beat his great swinging fist on his chest; his voice rolled and boomed from the depths. "I got those home-again blues." His conical skull swayed from side to side. "Home," he chanted, "knock on the door!"

"Lay off, nigger," snapped Anthony. "I'll have the carpenter in."

"Quail, he think he swim. Long way New York, Quail." Laughter exploded richly in the bunks.

"Quail, he feel water, he fear soap to come!"

Quail held onto the post. "Home, just as before," he moaned. "Home again, to roam no more. . . ."


Most of the late morning Mr. MacGillivray had a crew on the ash-ejector valve. It must have worked loose during the heavy weather while they were heaved-to earlier. By noon they had it tight again, but water was pouring smoothly into the stoke-hole by the bunker chutes. It slopped around the dog box and washed back and forth on the plates. Perhaps a bunker-hatch cover had gone and Mr. MacGillivray suggested this to the bridge. He did not know whether they had done anything about it or not but he had started a pump at half past ten and still needed it. In fact he would have used all his pumps but he had been ordered to empty the rest of the port ballast-tanks. Meanwhile he was clearing his bilge by not more than a foot an hour and the whole place was in a mess, with pressure falling off. It was useless to tell the fire-room to shake her up. The men worked resentfully with a psychological slowness in a flooded stoke-hole. Mr. MacGillivray wished often and audibly to God that they were on oil, independent of firemen with wet feet and trimmers who were constantly losing their rakes in the shallow water.

It was his only public concession to the annoyances of the situation, which were, to his mind, many. Among other things, he wouldn't get to luncheon and he had a nice crowd at his table, including two good-looking women who called him chief and knew a funny story when they heard one—well, that was the way it always worked, and probably they were seasick anyway. There would be plenty more meals when they got South and had nicer weather. At the moment it was still remarkably rough. Much rougher than there was any need for it to be, he decided, having gone above a moment for the purpose. Most of it was the half-witted way they handled the ship.

Half past three, declared the clock on the stairs which Anthony had just passed, moving down the port alleyway of the C deck. He was going aft to find out what had been done five minutes before by a green sea taken broad on the quarter. It pooped them with a shock like a hill falling aboard. Anthony could not figure it out—how, in view of wind, weather, and the *San Pedro's* course, it ever got there. He was extraordinarily tired. In this state, the ocean became almost personified; a purposeful and malicious agent, driving its heavy assaults to the unexpected and unguarded points. At the *San Pedro's* heavy stagger, Captain Clendening went out and looked aft. Obviously a boat had gone from the steerage superstructure, for one thing. The supports of the after-bridge were twisted. White water cascaded endlessly off the poop-deck as the fantail shook itself free. You could hear the descending crash all the way forward. He said without emphasis: "Find out what carried away, Mr. Bradell."

Anthony went, as smartly as he could make his aching legs move. He was certain that it would prove to have been particularly, wantonly, destructive. The steerage passengers were probably in a panic. In fact, there was no reason to suppose they hadn't lost a few people overboard. Anthony reviewed these possibilities in a stupor of resentment. A figure was approaching him in the alleyway and he faltered a moment, trying to calculate by the lethargic lurch of the tilted floor whether to pass right or left.

"Hello, Bradell," she said. "Such a nice day, isn't it?"

She moved a little with the shift underfoot, and managed, intentionally or not, to block the whole alleyway, so he had to halt. "Sorry," he said. "I've got to get aft."

"Listen, Bradell," she said. "Do something about this. Clara and tons of people are sick as dogs. And I can't even get a bath. The bath-steward says we aren't level enough. I'll be positively filthy if it keeps up many weeks." She regarded him with clear good humor and he saw that her eyes were blue. "You don't look well, Bradell," she continued critically. "Have a sleepless night? So did I. I couldn't get my mind off you. And the food is atrocious, such of it as stays on the table. It was bad enough before."

"Sorry," repeated Anthony. "Don't worry. Everything is all right."

All the woodwork creaked and cried out with the roll. She put a hand on his arm and said: "Good Lord, is it as bad as that?"

She seemed obscurely to cling to him, impeding his thought as well as his progress. He felt too tired to shake her off, so he said: "No danger at all. Everything is all right."

"Listen, Bradell," she begged. "Tell me how bad it is. I'll be simply furious if I find out afterward we almost sank and I didn't even know it. A girl has to have some kick out of life."

"Everything is all right," said Anthony, looking at her. She frowned a little, tightening the fingers on his arm.

"I thought at first there couldn't be anything wrong," she admitted, "because so many of the passengers were scared. Listen, Bradell, why don't you say it's the worst storm you've seen in ninety-seven years at sea, or something?"

"No danger," he said. "I've got to get aft."

"Bradell," she pleaded, "you don't hate me enough to go and drown all these innocent people too, do you? Besides, I told you I damn well didn't want to drown."

"All right," he exploded wearily. "You won't. Don't be such a fool."

Her face was getting whiter and whiter under the rouge. "Listen," she said, somewhat more huskily. "I've got plenty of nerve, but you have to tell me one thing." She hesitated an instant. "Bradell, are you sure that doctor man went ashore?"

"I've got to get aft," said Anthony, "I can't talk to you."

"Bradell, you weren't fooling me?"

"I can't talk to you," said Anthony. "Please step aside."

She moved, backing against the white-paneled wall, extending a lax arm on either side of her to grasp the handrail. She murmured: "Good-by, Bradell."

He passed her. Although he did not look, he could feel her still there, her dark head up, leaning against the wall mutely, her blue eyes on his retreating back.

In the wireless-room Smith, the first operator, regarded Morris without favor. Morris was on duty. He had, as

usual, the phones pushed off one ear. A cigarette nodded
up and down as he hummed to himself. His tobacco-dyed
forefinger kept the key in a vibrating, whining chatter—
QSU—QRN—QRU. . . . The *San Pedro's* WPRV went
on to the end. He locked his hands in back of his head
and sucked at the cigarette.

"Who was that?" asked Smith, still sleepy.

*"San Pablo."*

"We aren't reporting anything?"

"Having a fine time. Wish you were here. Want me to
write a poem, or tell 'em the one about the stuffed
monkeys?"

"It doesn't feel so good to me," said Smith. "Where did
we get all this water?"

"Elephant charged the camera," admitted Morris, delighted, "but I dropped him at twenty paces. He's in the
wastepaper basket."

"Funny boy, aren't you?" marveled Smith. "Are we all
right?"

"As advertised," agreed Morris. He drawled with relish,
gleeful: "These magnificent vessels are unsurpassed in comfort and luxury. Having been especially constructed for
tropical voyaging, the ventilation of every room is perfect
—just feel it," he invited, turning up his collar. "Running
water, too," he added, "in every room now. Some with
baths."

"Don't, I'll die!" grunted Smith.

"Appetizing meals to delight the keen appetites aroused
by the bracing sea air—" He seized a partly consumed
ham sandwich from the plate beside him. "Do take some
more caviar, count," he urged. "It will only be thrown
out."

"Say, listen," said Smith. "Is that all we get to eat?"

"That? You don't even get that. That's mine. Try and

find another. While you were absent they procured five tons of sea water somewhere at great expense and put them in the ranges. Didn't they consult you?"

"After the applause dies down, let's see the bridge orders."

"Help yourself," said Morris cordially. "The old man keeps wanting to know where the *San Pablo* is, as if I gave a damn! When I get them, he doesn't want them for anything. Their lad told me for God's sake to leave them alone. That shows how little he's been out. Nothing like a valve transmitter in unscrupulous hands, I always say. We'll bother them, if you want to know, from thirty-five to forty-five on twenty-one hundred continuous every hour for the rest of the night."

"What's the idea?"

"Oh, just a little thing I tossed off while I was waiting. It isn't finished yet, of course, but the old man certainly liked it."

"Listen, I'll relieve you now. Like a good sport, go down and get me a sandwich, will you?"

"Wrong," protested Morris.

"Listen, have I got to order you?"

"No, no, don't feel that way. Accidents happen."

"Go on, get up. You got a drag down there."

"Say, you certainly presume on your white hairs, Lord Algy," groaned Morris. "All together now; American Marconi Company, I love you!"

The narrow promenade around the fantail had lost a long section of rail. On the port side the Third-Class pantry had been flushed out clean. The door was carried away; every detachable object was swept through with the rail. For the moment it would be simpler to assume that no one had been on duty there, Anthony decided. He continued around the stern. Not a square inch of glass was left in any exposed window. The stewards would have to rope off the unprotected deck, and looking for them, he put his shoulder against the starboard entry doors.

Inside, the constricted stairs came up to the Third-Class lounge. Furniture consisted mainly of benches fastened to the walls, but there was a big table. This had torn out the pin of the stay-chain, overturning and scattering newspapers and old magazines on the linoleum, shining with dirty water. Forty faces, black or palely negroid, lifted to Anthony. The high, miserable storm of voices quailed a moment. Then the sight of his uniform cap drove up a louder wail; partly hysterical relief at finding they were not alone in the world, partly fresh panic at the appearance of authority, in most of their minds associated with disaster and unreasonable suffering to come.

Anthony endeavored to ignore them, but his rapid and accurate eye included them all. Some sat paralyzed, bundles of their poor possessions done up in sheets resting at their feet. Others had gotten inefficiently into lifebelts. One group appeared to be praying, led by a monstrous woman with a mustache. More practical, another group had procured several bottles.

"Steward!" Anthony called.

Not understanding him, most of them joined in, too; a general lamentation. The old woman with the mustache shrieked louder. The people with bundles laid hold of them. A man with a bottle tilted it up as far as it would go.

"Pipe down!" shouted Anthony. "Shut up! You're all right." He realized that they did not understand him. "No hay periculo! Basta! Basta!"

That exhausted his Spanish, but they understood at

least that he was trying to talk to them. With appalling suddenness a silence fell, marred on the edges by stifled groans and sobs. They swayed visibly toward him, all eyes fastened to him, all waiting for him to perform some miracle and save them.

"No hay periculo," repeated Anthony. "Esta bien."

His broken Spanish was worse than nothing. It frightened them more. The uncertainty of his accent, the inadequacy of his words, made everything he said improbable, sinister even. They were clearly cut off from the people who had them in charge, who had brought them to this extremity and alone could deliver them. The moaning swelled up again and Anthony shouted: "Doesn't any one speak English?"

White under his black skin one man said nervelessly: "What you like to say, señor?"

"Tell them to go back to their staterooms."

"No, no, mister," he wailed. "No, no. Room full of water. People sick. People scared. No, no."

"Tell them."

"No, no," he groaned. "Ship sink. People drown. Leave those here, mister."

"Where's the steward?"

"What you say, mister?"

"The steward!"

"No, no, mister. No, no."

"Where is the man with the white coat?" Anthony shouted.

"Some gone. Some sick in room. Some under bed."

"Where?" snapped Anthony. "Show me."

"No, no. I stay here, mister. No, no."

Anthony did not move, but simple savagery must have shown in his face, for the man cowered away into the

corner, backing against people who parted struggling to
keep far from Anthony. Their shrieks swelled up again.
The whole frail fabric of human relationships melted now
in a mess of paralyzed muscle and brain and will. More
shocking than the most murderous resistance, they became simply dead weight. They were lumps weighing some
hundred and fifty pounds, too yielding to grasp, too mis-
shapen to handle. Anthony stood dark-eyed and stiff-
faced. He wanted to plant his feet in these quivering gelat-
inous heaps. He was shaken to the bottom—indeed there
was no bottom, only the unthinkable abyss of human impotence opened under him. His brain, suspended over it,
counseled him merely to kill, trample them down, destroy
them, before their shocking contagion destroyed him. The
blood beat up and filmed over his eyes, and he was saved
by a quick, idiotic irrelevancy. He recognized that he
was seeing red; that there was such a thing, no figure of
speech, but a bloody mist. The childish surprise of it
unsprung his nerves. He turned stiffly, grasped the rail of
the stairs, and, putting one foot before another, descended.
At the bottom his voice came like a croak, but he cleared
it and shouted: "Steward!"

A figure appeared uncertainly at the end of the little
passage. "Where are the others?" Anthony asked.

"In the pantry, they were," faltered this man, glassy-
eyed.

Three, maybe four, men gone, swept off and smothered
somewhere in the broken wake, was a fact, literal and
sharp. At once the misery of wetness and fear, the noise
above, like animals crowded in a dangerous pen, became
a simpler thing, pitiable. If, a moment ago, Anthony could
have wished them all scoured out by the hard sea, buried
away and obliterated, now he felt only their wretched hu-

manity, their common helplessness against the inhuman ocean.

"Poor devils," he murmured. The man's enormous eyes looked up at him. "All right," Anthony said. "We can't do anything now. Buck up!"

The man opened his mouth and no sound came out, but finally he said: "Yes, sir."

"Unlock the passage-door there. I'll get some men down to you. Everything is all right. Go above and don't let any one out. Half the rail's carried away."

"Yes, sir." The steward spoke more securely. He at least had the outlines of a discipline, however irregular or casual. This framework propped him up a little, made him firm enough to grasp. Once grasped, the current of command galvanized him. His chin rose, his shaking ceased. "Yes, sir," he repeated quickly.

"Look alive," said Anthony. "We'll probably be out of this before dark."


At nine o'clock Mr. MacGillivray and his fourth engineer finished work on the extra pump. Designed for blowing ashes or supplying water to the deck fire-lines, they turned it on the stubbornly making bilge, broke the joint connection and fitted on a screen filter. That raised their available horse-power to about two hundred. As there was never anything wrong with the gear in an engine-room ruled by Mr. MacGillivray, the pumps were better than seventy per cent efficient. Together they sucked up a ton of water a minute, heaved it thirty feet from the level of the fire-room plates, and dumped it over the side.

The chief viewed this arrangement, satisfied. He did not know where so much water could be coming from, but

he was, he felt sure, more than a match for it. He would
have his bilges dry before morning. If it came to that, he
could and would pump out the whole blasted ocean.
He'd have no dirty water in his department.

Presently he went above to clean up. Soaping his big
hands, he felt rather grumpy. As he got older he tended
more and more to regard sailors, deck officers, as a not
very necessary nuisance. If they ever developed a tenth of
the efficiency he demanded and received from his person-
nel, from his main plant, from every fitting and auxiliary,
there might be some sense in shipping. As it was, you took
the finest turbines made by man and put them in a tin
scow run by a lot of damn fools who filled it with water,
ran it on its side and near shook the lagging off. He was
tired now, but he certainly wasn't turning in until they got
a grip on things. Though the sea was moderating, the *San
Pedro* rolled heavily. The list was to twenty degrees and
he didn't believe what water he had below was doing it.

Returning to his office, he put on his uniform coat
and settled at the desk, his hands folded on his belly, his
porcelain-blue eyes brooding. He was there when the
alleyway door opened and he saw that at last the captain
had come below. Mr. MacGillivray got to his feet. Mr.
Bradell had entered with the old man. He stood at his
elbow, as though he were helping him to walk, and the
chief noticed that Captain Clendening moved heavily, without determination.

"Evening, captain," he said shortly.

"How is it?" said Captain Clendening at last.

"We're all right," Mr. MacGillivray nodded. "Got three
pumps on. Have us dry pretty soon. Can't we do something about this list? Throws my lubrication off. Burn out
a bearing somewhere, I wouldn't be surprised." Actually

he would be stunned with surprise. He had an extraordinary extra-sense for developing friction; it would be a clever bearing that burnt out in his engine-room.

"Where do you think the water's coming from, MacGillivray?" Captain Clendening asked.

Mr. MacGillivray pulled his loose chin. "It's black water," he said. "Must come through the coal. Don't suppose we sprung a plate?"

"I don't know," said Captain Clendening.

Mr. MacGillivray looked at him sharply. "Aren't you trying to find out?" he asked.

"Since about four this morning," interposed Mr. Bradell, "we haven't done anything else, chief."

"Now, if I were you, son," said Mr. MacGillivray, "I'd get myself in overalls and poke about the port bunkers. You can get in from the shelter-deck. Take an electric flashlight and keep it dry——"

"I'll give Bradell his orders, Mr. MacGillivray," said Captain Clendening.

"Just offering a suggestion," said Mr. MacGillivray, his mouth pouting out from the hanging folds of cheek. "Seems to me about time something was done."

Captain Clendening's lumpy jaw sagged down and forward. His mustache stiffened. "By God, sir," he roared, "I'll have you understand, Mr. MacGillivray, that I am in command of this ship. When I want your suggestions, I'll ask for them!"

"Very good," snapped Mr. MacGillivray. "And now I'll step below, with your permission, and get on with more important matters."

He turned his back on them. The clear snorts of his breathing sounded above the roar of the engine-room shaft for a moment. He stumped down the steel steps.

Captain Clendening swallowed audibly. "Boy?" he said.

"Yes, sir," said Anthony.

Captain Clendening made an uneasy gesture. "Go down, boy," he said. "My apologies to Mr. MacGillivray. Sort of nervous, boy. Guts are no good. Got to take care of myself. Tell him I appreciate his hard work. Tell him I rely on him absolutely and I hope he'll see fit to overlook my—my"—he faltered—"my language, that is."

"Yes, sir," said Anthony. The captain's mouth worked a little and Anthony hesitated, not knowing if he were finished.

The captain's eyes came back to him, focussed harder a moment. "Mr. Bradell!"

"Yes, sir."

"Perhaps you can tell me who is in command of this vessel?"

"You are, sir," said Anthony, dumfounded.

"Thank you. When I give an order, I want it obeyed. What are you standing here for? Look alive, sir! I'll have no oil-tanker customs on this ship!"

# 4

Miro had gone below when Mr. Bradell told him to turn in. Wind, weather; noise, no matter how relentless; discomfort very severe, he could ignore when he was ready to sleep. Now, long past midnight, he knew no such thing had disturbed him. His eyes open in the dark, he was at once alert, roused from within. Believing that an angel watched over him, he recognized instantly what had happened. This invisible being, who saw all and knew all, had bent down suddenly. Her tall shadow fell on him, her great wings fanned him.

He was not perturbed, nor was he hurried, though it could mean only that danger had become at last real and imminent. Perhaps all day danger had been mounting, like fluid in a pressure tube. Now it had crossed a mark and its crossing touched off tremendous alarms. His inquiring physical senses assured him that to every appearance nothing had changed. Slow and steady, the hammer of the engines at half-speed and time continued; the *San Pedro* rolled sluggishly; water forward bumped and crashed. A sound of movement and still calm enough voices came from the working alleyway. All the greater reason to find out, if he could, what subtler or more sinister change had caught his angel's sleepless eye, made her reach down and rouse him.

He had not taken off his boots, so he came at once to his feet. The occasional lights of the narrow wet passage, tilted badly by the list, burned dim in their heavy cups of misted glass. He proceeded aft to the working alleyway and saw to his astonishment a dozen men from the steward's department. The half-door, he observed immediately, had carried away altogether. The carpenter was there, trying to rig a new one of boards and canvas. It was not completed and only partly in place, so when they leaned far on the list the sea came right in. One had a momentary staggering glimpse of their dull lights spilling into the void, winking on fathomless black swells almost under foot. Coming back enough to conceal this ugly phenomenon, the water already shipped surged to starboard like a miniature tidal wave. It went above the knees of the carpenter and his mate, busy with their boards.

Mr. Driscoll had been absent a moment before, but Miro saw him now, buttoned up in his bridge coat, his face remarkably white in the bad light. He picked out Miro in the shadow beyond and said: "Quartermaster?"

Miro answered, greatly relieved to find the chief officer in such alert charge.

"See if you can rout out some more men here. Get a lot of men. Any men you can." Mr. Driscoll supported himself with one hand on the clammy wall as the *San Pedro* went over and the half-door framed the black sea like a steep floor. "Wait," he said.

"Yes, sir."

"Report to the bridge first. Tell the captain that the situation doesn't seem to improve. You might ask if it would be possible for him to step below here a moment. I —er—" He became conscious of the deadly silence of the men listening. "Hurry up," he jerked out. "Get on with it."

Mr. Driscoll, then, was worried, too. Miro, in point of private fact, had small respect for Mr. Driscoll as a seaman. He did not believe now that Mr. Driscoll knew what ought to be done, nor even how to go about whatever substitute for the right thing he might have in mind. Mounting the inside stairs to the chart-room, Miro decided to report to Mr. Bradell first. Mr. Bradell could tell him what to do, and once sure himself, he might discover some way to modify Mr. Driscoll's designs.

He found this intention defeated, however. He appeared quietly in the door, and was dismayed to see the wheel-house almost crowded. Both Mr. Eberly and Mr. Sheedy were standing by. Young Mr. Fenton and the third officer were close together in the corner. The fifth officer, Mr. Eberly's junior, balanced himself restlessly with the roll, looking at the ceiling. Mr. Bradell, his arms folded tight, the brim of his cap down over his forehead, stood beside the engine-room telegraph. The helmsman's eyes swung furtively from the binnacle to the rudder indicator and then sideways, as though appealing to Mr. Bradell.

Unnoticed in the door behind, Miro considered them one after another. They were all tired, yet they were all alert too, quiet and composed, but obviously mystified. One could deduce that they were here because they had been ordered up. They had not been told why, they had not been told what to do. No one spoke; they simply waited. It was, in its inept, mute, rather bewildered way, magnificent, and Miro appreciated this. Here was a very superior form of *tela,* a splendid, passive morale, the supreme ability to remain motionless and to appear calm; to stand endlessly ready for no one knew what.

Since Mr. Bradell had the watch, it would be impossible to speak to him. Miro hesitated soundlessly, considering to whom he should speak. At this moment the port door onto the open bridge moved and Captain Clendening came in.

His face under the electric light was positively lifeless, but it had a surface shine from the spray on it. His eyes were so far swollen that they seemed to wink craftily out of slits. He stood heavy and clumsy in his wet bridge coat a moment. All glances had gone to him, but they wavered now, went away. There was a slight simultaneous movement of lips and eyes returning to careful impassivity. Mr. Bradell never budged, had not looked.

Paying no attention to his waiting officers, Captain Clendening kept his face toward Miro. "Yes?" he said.

"Chief officer reports, sir," said Miro. "Mr. Driscoll wants to know if you can step below, sir."

There was a general restrained stir, but no other sound.

"No," said Captain Clendening. "Tell him to carry on."

The helmsman let his brown, nervous face turn. "Helm!" said Mr. Bradell. The helmsman's eyes jerked front.

In his gray-yellow face Captain Clendening's eyeballs flickered. A slight muscular contraction shook the thick cheeks. "Turn in, Mr. Eberly," he said. "Get some sleep. Won't want you after all." He jerked his head toward the third and fifth officers. "You, too," he said. "Turn in. Mr. Sheedy, report to the chief officer."

They all moved immediately in the grateful release of definite orders.

"Quartermaster?"

"Yes, sir."

"Find out from the wireless-room where the *San Pablo* is."

"Yes, sir."

"Mr. Bradell?"

"Yes, sir."

"Can you carry on a little longer?"

"Yes, sir."

Miro was out through the chart-room. In his ears repeated and repeated the mechanical "Yes, sir," "Yes, sir." It lost all alacrity, all smart and competent obedience. The phrase hammered and hammered. Under the senseless impact, the frame-work of observation—the vital initiative, the intelligence to see clearly and do quickly—cracked, crumbled to dust. Discipline, directed coöperation, ceased here to have any virtue. Habit betrayed the will and debauched the brain. Physically, the lips might stiffen with reluctance, the voice almost fail, but the mind in its extremity knew only one reply. To disaster, to stupid folly, to terrible peril which might yet be averted or resisted; to the advance of death itself, the mind acquiescent, drugged with a phrase, answered only, "Yes, sir."

Wet wind hit Miro in the face. Beneath his feet the deck tilted away. He caught a handrail; he saw the dim bands of the *San Pedro's* funnel stagger in the dark. He knew now that the *San Pedro* was certainly foundering, however slowly, and that most of those she carried might be lost.


Tuckerton, New Jersey. East Moriches, Long Island. All night rain has fallen on the Atlantic coast. Dawn is up, wet from the eastern ocean, but before six o'clock the sullen skies were breaking. Heavy smell of wet trees, wide wet meadows, and the warm damp earth spread everywhere; through country streets, silent, but brighter; into the quiet open windows of houses still asleep. There followed presently a thin noise of bird song. Over the edge of the world, just about level with the drenched tree-tops, poured out the sun. Its flat, enormous shafts struck resplendent across the Eastern States. At Tuckerton, and at East Moriches, far higher than trees, slender and rigid against the fine dissolving blue, stood up the skeleton towers of the coastal wireless stations.

Under them, in the power-houses, in the offices and operating rooms, some of the lights were turned off. Shifts of operators and engineers changed. The great generators, not requiring relief, spun on, subdued; but there was a sound of released voices on the beautiful air outside. An early train had tossed off New York papers, and men walking slowly home to bed lit cigarettes, looked at them, and saw there was no news worth reading.

Inside, the morning reliefs were settling down. Outside, soundless, invisible, humanly indetectable, the serene, the golden June air swelled, grew full with rising volume; the racing, screaming whine of code communication; broadcasting voices clearly relayed; early music.

At seven-fifteen, into these crowded currents which carried the immense record of the awakened world, cut faintly the *San Pedro's* CQ—a thin plea, staccato with foreboding. From far off the Virginia Capes they were nagging at human attention; *everybody listen*. At Tuckerton, at East Moriches, the emergency operators stirred, attentive, mildly curious, as a half-hour silence settled. Just before eight o'clock came the SOS. By eight o'clock the Brooklyn Navy Yard was suspending all radio traffic. Over the whole of Eastern North America the air was abruptly emptied and into this immense void the *San Pedro* called again, small and solitary; faded out; called once more, appealing now to the Naval Compass Station at Cape May for her true bearings.

They heard it on the largest ship in the world; the white vessels of the United Fruit Company, many-decked Clyde liners, a dozen ships of the Caribbean and Southern trade, picked it up, calculating the scores of separating miles. Slow, dogged, steaming stockily, the Japanese freighter *Toledo Maru* halted a hundred miles away and came heavily about; from the North Atlantic steamship lanes a moderately fast Cunarder broke, turned south, forcing her draft; a German boat, farther east, bound for New York, turned too. Just over the horizon a small sugar tramp from Cuba came abreast, passed the *San Pedro,* crawled patiently on, not being equipped with wireless.


Captain Clendening's eyeballs were finely netted with scarlet veins. There was a silver stubble of beard over his square cheeks. Beneath his short white mustache his mouth opened and shut, sucking in the cool air. He held onto the shutter of the open wheel-house window, and the cumbersome seas, whipping up the tilted well-deck forward, staggering into the port half-doors, were gray with advanced morning. The *San Pedro,* resisting them, shook him back and forth on his feet, but he held on. He held the tighter, for he did not wish to turn around; he felt, insistent, the need to look back, to survey the boat-deck again, but he put it off a moment while his head wabbled. "Got to take care of myself," he murmured, for he knew that he was very sick, ought to be in bed. In answer he held himself still tighter, harder, while he did turn and look back. He realized then that he could not see anything unless he went out on the open bridge end. There was, however, a quartermaster gazing at him. The man's eyes were dark, sad, deep as wells. "Order to abandon, sir?" he said softly.

Captain Clendening was stunned. He opened his mouth to roar, but his throat failed him. He could not believe that he had understood; that on his own bridge a quartermaster could be offering him a suggestion. He breathed harder, he held tighter, as though he were climbing a vertical slope. The situation was so outrageous and amazing that, still speechless, he wondered if it might not have been his imagination, for the man was saying normally, like any quartermaster: "Chief officer reports starboard boats impractical, sir."

He hesitated and Captain Clendening, his mouth tight, his eyes hard ahead, continued to look at him.

"Mr. Bradell asked me to say, sir, that port boats could be dropped in the lee and get off. May he reverse orders, sir?"

Captain Clendening studied him, studied his brown clear skin and melancholy liquid eyes, knew that he had noticed him often before, that this was a reliable man. "What's your name?" he asked.

"Miro, sir," answered the quartermaster. There was a sudden brightening of his eyes as though he were about to weep.

They were all inordinately sensitive, these Southerners; particularly, intelligent ones; Captain Clendening knew. He modified his tone a little. "Don't you know how to behave on the bridge, boy?" he said. "Look alive and speak when you're spoken to."

"Yes, sir," said Miro.

"Well, what did you want?"

"About life-boat stations, sir. Mr. Bradell—"

"I gave no orders about boats," said Captain Clendening, his voice thick in his ears. "What are you talking about?"

The man's deep sad eyes with the far-away glint of tears stayed on him steadily. "You will remember, sir," he said. His voice was mild, very gentle, but distinct. "You ordered Mr. Bradell and Mr. Driscoll to turn to on the boats."

"I sent Mr. Bradell forward," said Captain Clendening. "What's he doing with the boats?"

"Yes, sir," assented the soft clear voice. "That was afterward. He has gone forward now, sir."

"Why didn't you report at once? I'll have no tampering with—"

He found, to his amazement, that he must have been interrupted. "I try to report, sir, for ten—twenty minutes. I have been right here, sir. I do not think that you have heard me." The man's face was a still, tragic mask with the small deep pools of the eyes. "Boats have broken on the side, sir. It is too—"

"Officers," said Captain Clendening, "will carry out

their orders to the best of their ability." He extended a hand. "I want to go onto the bridge," he said.

Miro came close, more like a sudden close-up in a motion-picture than ordinary movement. Miro's hard, neatly muscled shoulder steadied Captain Clendening. Very sure-footed, Miro calculated the movement of the ship, moving with it, and they were out, under the terrible white light of the pale sky. Captain Clendening shook off Miro's support, holding the rail and watching the concerted movement about the life-boats. His mouth was full of spittle, tasting brazen, or bitter, and he swallowed steadily, trying to get rid of it.

Now some one else had appeared at the wheel-house door. Captain Clendening tightened his jaw and said: "You have your orders, Mr. Fenton. Be good enough to carry them out." The quartermaster was still gazing at him, so he added, enraged at last by the implacable sadness of the eyes: "Get that man out of here, Mr. Fenton. I'll have him in irons if he leaves his post again."

He heard Mr. Fenton's voice: ". . . get some of them away, sir?" and it occurred to him that he might not have spoken aloud in reference to the quartermaster. He saw no use in repeating it. To Mr. Fenton he said automatically: "You will await an order for general abandonment. How are the passengers?"

"Mr. Eberly and Mr. Sheedy are in charge, sir. Women and children mustered up. All behaving well."

"Right," said Captain Clendening. "We'll have no *La Bourgogne* business here."

Still a third man had appeared. He recognized this one as from the wireless-room. He had in his hand several papers. His voice awoke in an animated drawl. "Yes, yes," said Captain Clendening sharply. He did not want to listen to this, so he took the scribbled reports from the young man. "Carry on," he nodded, anxious to get rid of them.


In the wireless-room Smith was at the key. "On the coil now," he said to Morris, returning. "When are we going to abandon?"

Morris lit a cigarette, propped himself in the tilted corner. He employed his free hand thoughtfully, scratching his red hair. "Nobody knows," he hummed, "and nobody seems to care."

"Listen," said Smith. "Don't wisecrack. I don't mind telling you I want to live. How's the old man?"

"He's all right," said Morris. He hesitated an instant, examining the palms of his hands. Then he wiped them deliberately on the seams of his uniform trousers. "He looks pretty bad. You don't lose your ship every day, now I come to think of it, but he's playing ball."

"What's he say?"

"Nothing," answered Morris. "Which seems to me to be about right. They stove in another boat just now." His face stirred, became lively, grinning. "Pretty soon we'll have to take off our shoes and stockings and wade; that is, those not otherwise engaged. I'll flip you to see who does the Casabianca stunt. We'll count Couch out, since he wouldn't be on duty anyway. Where is he, having a quiet nap?"

"Out with Mr. Driscoll. He's had some experience with boats. Well—"

"If he has, he's the only one," said Morris. "I could tell you a good joke, only it might upset you. Let's have a half-dollar."

"I'll stay," said Smith. "I'm the senior operator."

"You're sure hell on heroism," commented Morris, enlivened, "but I've only one cigarette left, so I might as well drown. Furthermore, what did I happen to find but a quart of Bacardi, which will take away the taste of salt water something wonderful. I'll even give you a drink if you'll lend me your boy-scout knife."

"Now, shut up!" said Smith sharply. "Don't get all worked up. Everything's all right. We'll float for eight hours at least and by three o'clock——"

"You must have heard Mr. Eberly talking to the passengers," admired Morris. "That's the good joke. I was going to tell you. He has them all down on the promenade-deck, and since they don't know him very well—some of them have barely met him—they think he knows what it's all about."

"And I suppose you know a hell of a lot more?"

"I know this," said Morris modestly. "If we don't stop leaning over the rail, we're going to capsize. Thank God I'm not a seaman; I'd miss all the fun of expecting it."

"You aren't so damn humorous," said Smith.

"Get off the key," suggested Morris, "and let me hand these boys a few sad brave remarks."

"Don't be an ass!" snapped Smith. "What juice we have we'll keep. Hang on, I got the Jap boat again."

He penciled down letters in silence. "You didn't bring back any new bearings, did you?" he asked Morris over his shoulder. "They've got a ten-cent outfit with no direction finder."

"Shoot them something snappy for a come-on," begged Morris. "Don't be a Western Union messenger all your life."

"Shut up," said Smith. His key awoke, and Morris, reading it off, translated freely: " 'Bad enough here old man position ship in hardly stay receive please hurry—' That's right," he applauded. "Probably they were wondering

about that last part. Probably they didn't know whether to
hurry or to stop and do a little fishing."

"For God's sake, shut up!" shouted Smith.

"Sorry," claimed Morris. "Didn't mean to spoil our last
happy hours together. Well, before we get any more good
news, I'll flip you two out of three for that space on the
Memorial in Battery Park, the bottle, and all your cigarettes. Come on, boy, think of your lovin' wife."

Smith said glumly: "Well, at any rate I haven't got that
to worry about."

Morris's great grin of derision shone on him. "It would
be horrible," he nodded; "I expect you couldn't keep your
mind off her if you had one. Never mind, think of your
children in all parts of the world, then. What'll it be?
Heads?"


Mr. Eberly carried a revolver in his pocket but he found
no use for it. On the appalling tilt of the promenade-deck
one felt unpleasantly shut in, seeing only the pale heavens,
the fast eastward drift of the melting scud to starboard;
only the long jostling slide of gray water getting green to
port. From above came the dull sound of boots and men
working, which was comforting. So was the undisturbed
solidity of the ship. Even at this awkward angle the deck
underfoot was firm as rock; the steel walls, white-painted,
the windows, the heavy doors, looked strong and normal
enough.

Mr. Eberly had all the passengers on deck now; the
women and children in one compact group forward, ready
for the boats which he presumed would be first down. At
the after-rail, by the closed stairs, Mr. Sheedy waited,
holding frankly an iron stanchion. He was watching the
big Negroes of the black gang, who had either come up

anyway or been sent up. They gathered, sullen, restless but impotent, about the hatch covers. They hadn't yet made any real movement to approach the promenade-deck. Mr. Eberly, moving with the aid of lines that he had rigged himself, passed up and down watching everybody; the groups of men smoking with affected calm; the confused herd of women where occasionally a child cried. He told them—he was careful not to do it too often—that there was absolutely no danger, and it was fine to see how they behaved; resigned, patient, doing exactly as they were asked. He had directed them to dress as warmly as possible, and he made sure that they had their ludicrous, bulky lifebelts on properly. Some of them managed to regard their appearance as amusing, and fortunately they were too ignorant to make any protest about a delay which Mr. Eberly himself found inexplicable, nerve-racking. Once he went inside with unhurried calm, waited a few minutes, and came out. "Assistance alongside in about an hour," he announced, with the well-sustained implication that he had been to the wireless-room.

Mr. Sheedy occasionally said, addressing the invisible deck aft: "Take your foot off the ladder, nigger, or you'll get a broken head." Then there was a faint stir, lasting only a minute; a slight acknowledgment of this obvious hint that some other people were not quite so calm. But they all knew, they had read or been told plenty of times, that the one real danger in matters like this was simply panic. Certainly they could see no other, now that they were used to the ship's position. They believed that men who understood the situation were doing everything possible to get them off quickly and safely; they had, in fact, nothing to worry about so long as they stayed quiet and did what Mr. Eberly directed them to do.

"Everything," asserted Mr. Eberly, who was still trying to explain to himself why Mr. Driscoll wasted so much time on the starboard boats, when it would have seemed fairly simple to Mr. Eberly to let go the port ones, "is all right."

Driven by his consuming anxiety, he finally did find a reason. The captain must consider it wiser to try to get off as many of the starboard boats as they could first. The port ones might be handled somewhat more expeditiously if later it proved that they were pressed for time. The idea, he told himself, had much to be said for it. He was heartened, too, by the indication it gave of confidence on the bridge that they would float a long while. With the impassivity of good discipline he refrained from sending above to make inquiries which could only be useless and ridiculous. "Try to be patient just a little longer," he requested earnestly. "I know this isn't very comfortable, but there's no danger. The sun," he added with a sort of cheerfulness, "will be out in a minute."

From the well-deck forward Anthony could see Captain Clendening's stubborn, hatless white head against the sky. It was the one human detail in the confusion of the *San Pedro's* superstructure. Insistently under Anthony's eyes the Negroes crouched against the cased automobiles. Their wide feet clung like stunted hands to the rivets of the deck-plates. Cords bulged out of their black necks; sweat trickled flashing under the wool on their skulls. Their enormous paws locked over levers; black hills of muscle humped across their straining shoulders; their eyes rolled white, their thick lips contracted.

Anthony looked at them through a fluctuating reddish mist. Weariness tightened his throat in rhythmic cramping retches. He would have spewed out his empty stomach if he could. Both his hands he had to keep behind him so he

would not break an hysterical fist on the black stencil of
an Indian's head, outstanding with the maker's name on
the side of the case.

After a while he realized that men and muscle couldn't
do it. They would never get that case over the side. It
must be wedged. He cupped his raw hands and screamed
to the bridge: "Let me go below and make MacGillivray
give me steam on the winches, sir!"

He couldn't tell whether Captain Clendening heard him,
whether the old man could hear anything, or understand
if he did hear. The white head, stubbornly held up, wagged
a little.

Anthony turned. "Drop that. Get up number two starboard boom—" There was no one, he saw, to whom he
could safely delegate authority if he wanted intelligent action, but he picked out a man finally. "You," he said,
"stand by to let in the valves. We'll get steam."

At the end, the Negro called Packy released his lever.
His big hands pulled it out. One moment he poised on the
tilted deck, his head sunk, his black jaw swung out. Water
raced up to his feet; his shoulders balanced. The steel bar
drove like a battering-ram into the Indian's stenciled profile. Anthony wiped his forehead. His voice was thin as
water. "Lay off that, nigger!"


The wood had splintered at the terrible impact. Pallid sun-
shine from the aching white sky with the washed clouds
moving fell through the broken boards, winked on nickel,
on smooth cream-colored enamel. That's an expensive car
we're throwing away, thought Anthony.

He had removed his shoes to stand more securely. His
feet, cold and wet in his torn socks, gave him a good grip

on the slanting deck. The echo of the steel door closed behind him, and he forced himself to trot through the water in the alleyway. It caught his ankles and splashed at his knees; his unprotected heels falling hit his spine sickening jolts; and jarred beyond endurance, he had to stop, putting a hand, somehow worked raw, against the wall. He might have slept a moment, on his feet, to his shins in cold water, for he started, almost falling; remembered where he was going.

Under a raw, thin fog of vapor the engine-room depths formed an infernal swimming-pool. Like monster green hogsheads the turbine cases rose in a fantastic steel swamp. Incredible vegetation flowered; white piping; flattened-out layers of open-work footways. Stairs edged with brass rail plunged down, leading nowhere. Heavy tanks; pistons in a stiff paralysis of the final failure of almost all the auxiliary systems; transparent oil-cups with the oil at an angle in them; everything seemed to have changed places in a mechanical anarchy. Below, water moved about regularly, swaying to the sluggish roll. The engine-room shaft echoed like a sea cave. Choking with a hundred tons of brine in their throats the pumps groaned up to Anthony. Electric lights fluctuated, winked on the dirty sliding surface, steadied as the *San Pedro* came back. Anthony stumbled down the iron slant of the ladder.

There was Mr. MacGillivray. He had the fire-room door tied back, and the lock-door beyond fastened, too. He braced himself between them, his eyes on the indicator dials and the bridge signal. Sometimes the water came almost to his waist. Vapor slipped out steadily above his head, licking the upper jamb. Anthony missed a step, scraped his shin open, saw the bright blood run on his foot before he landed in the water. "Chief!"

Mr. MacGillivray snatched his arm. Anthony shouted above the catch and gasp of the pumps: "I've got to have steam."

Mr. MacGillivray's hanging cheeks were set into a cold calm. Unavoidably retreating, he had lost almost everything, but bitterly, step by step, he gave way in grim good order, contesting each point with the invading ocean. His obdurate old face was wary, undismayed. Anthony asked: "How much steam have you got, chief?"

Mr. MacGillivray's eyes came down from the dials. "Eighty pounds!" he shouted. "The center boiler's just gone. Listen to it!"

Over came the *San Pedro,* heavy and deliberate, rushing water into the hot fire-box. It sounded like the crash of thin metal sheets. The outlet valves whistled harder in the darkness. Mr. MacGillivray shook his finger at the fire-room. "To their necks, some of them," he roared. "We can't stay much longer."

Anthony swayed against him, looking through. A naked black back with prodigious arms bent to ease down a coal-bucket. Water swayed toward its armpits. In the upper corner a door came wide, and violent yellow light spurted in shattered columns across the liquid surface. A great shadow moved; coal crashed in, iron rang on iron, and the light went out. Up came a white back this time, another bucket.

"Electricity gone there!" roared the chief. "Go everywhere in a minute. Tell the old man. The telephone doesn't work."

The black figure with the dangling arms waded past. His face, his conical skull swayed into the light; he grinned; he swung his apelike arm and wagged the hand up and down. A faint boom-boom came from his chest. "Home," he moaned, "knock on the door. . . ."

"My God," said Anthony, shocked, "he's singing."

"Sure! He's crazy!" shouted Mr. MacGillivray. "No one who wasn't crazy would be here. He's the only nigger left."

Anthony swallowed. "Give me pressure on a winch, chief. I got to get some cases over."

MacGillivray stared at him, open-mouthed. He laid a hand on his shoulder and shook him. "Wake up!" he roared. "Come to! You can't use your booms in this list. Tie 'em down before you hurt some one."

"I can try," Anthony said, "I got to—"

"You cannot!" bellowed MacGillivray, his amazement melted in anger. "Hell and damnation, where are your brains, boy? Are you all crazy? You aren't at dock! Did the old man put that up to you?"

"Maybe I can work it," protested Anthony. "We've got to get those motors off. We—"

"Never mind them. You go up and find my fire-room crew. Tell the old man I got to have my men back." He shook Anthony's arm with a sort of fury. "Tell him they left. Tell him I got my engineers firing. Tell him if he wants to float to make those niggers come back here. Tell the old man we can't keep steam—tell him to come the hell down here himself!"

"He can't," shouted Anthony. "He's sick. He hasn't been to bed since Saturday night. What do you expect?"

"He's got no business to be sick," yelled MacGillivray. "Tell him I said so. Tell him we're foundering. Don't he give a damn? Don't he know we could capsize any minute? He'd lose every soul aboard. Just like that!" Mr. MacGillivray's loose fingers snapped soundless in the uproar. "Isn't he getting his passengers off?"

"We're doing everything we can," said Anthony. "We—"

"You are like hell!" roared MacGillivray. "Who's in command? The old man? He's dead to the world. Had him on the phone an hour ago and he didn't know what he was talking about! Why don't Driscoll take over? Why don't you take over? Are you so damn dumb you think you're going to float forever?"

"He's the master on this vessel," said Anthony. "As long as he's on the bridge giving orders, in the deck department we obey them. When we're ordered to abandon, we'll abandon. Meanwhile we keep our mouths shut."

Mr. MacGillivray stared at him. Then he spat hard into the dirty water in front of Anthony. "Get out of here, brat! Believe me, if I was a sailor, I'd rather be drowned than have to tell people afterward what I was doing all morning. Jesus, I hope some of you get off alive!"

Anthony turned, but Mr. MacGillivray caught his shoulder suddenly. "Listen," he roared. "Tell the old man! Get it into him! Ask what he's doing with four hundred human beings somebody's going to want from us afterward. Tell him for Christ's sake use his head—"

Miro, still on the bridge, waiting for any further orders Captain Clendening might have, could not imagine what the men on the well-deck forward had in mind. He watched them release a boom from its cradle. Then they stood a moment apparently arguing. Then with a sort of feverish violence, they scrambled above, all laid hold on the cable, and struggling hard brought the boom up, jerk by jerk. It tilted, staggered, mounted uncertain toward the perpendicular. What must surely be the idiocy of this performance did not surprise Miro so much as the energy with which they went about it. They might, of course, be contemplating something which he did not understand, but he noted that Mr. Bradell was absent, and it seemed more likely that they were acting on their own initiative.

Not speaking, for he knew that the captain would not hear him, he came close and pointed insistently until Captain Clendening looked. There was a long silence, and suddenly the captain, shaking his head a little, roared out: "On the fo'castle! Down that boom! What the devil is going on?"

Below, they wavered. Black faces turned. Out of the concealment of the deck-house under them came Mr. Bradell now, and he, too, turned. The boom hovered in a broken semicircle, balanced dizzily, went into a drunken side movement.

"Look alive, sir!" screamed Miro.

The boom, released, came too fast. With a blind, inert precision it swung farther left; the iron-sheathed timber struck like a well-directed club out of the anonymous skies. It knocked Mr. Bradell's poised figure ten feet into the scuppers. Up to them came the final crash of the demolished tip.

Captain Clendening opened his mouth and shut it. He shook his head and said: "Quartermaster?"

"Yes, sir," said Miro.

"Who was that?"

"Mr. Bradell, sir."

"Bradell," said Captain Clendening. "Bradell." He turned his head, continuing sharp and clearer: "Quartermaster."

"Yes, sir," said Miro, whiter.

"See about him." Captain Clendening's mustache worked stiffly. "Don't report back here. If he's alive, get him into a boat. Don't come back here. Get him away, get him off this ship. We're foundering."

"Yes, sir."

Left alone, Captain Clendening was quietly aware of death like a man beside him. He thought of his lungs bursting with sea water, a final agony of suffocation. This his body recoiled from, his gullet tightened, bitter saliva filling his mouth. He looked about carefully, as though there might be somewhere he could go; but it was a minute, never-completed gesture, for a habit of thought, an automatic pride, interrupted him. He was exposed, on the bridge; people could see him. The slugging of his heart, too large now for his chest, he could not control, but that was hidden. He knew perfectly how he had to die, and they did, too. He wished that they might for a moment face it; he would like to know—he was distracted, not ironic—if death would still seem so proper, so necessary, to them.

There his acuter senses broke down self-defensively. An anesthetic of poorer comprehension, a sort of mental stupor took off the momentary keen edge, veiled the face and fear of death. Deliberately, his hands heavy and inaccurate, he buttoned his bridge coat, tugged it into place. He made some motions to smooth the wrinkles from the sleeves, brushing the gold braid. After several uncertain efforts he picked up his uniform cap, and this, too, he brushed off, hitting it with his numb hand once or twice. Then he put it carefully on his head, brought the visor down, a stiff, somehow heartening, line across his vision. He stood as straight as he could, supporting himself when necessary on the rail.

From the south the sea was traveling in long swells. Miro, braced against the backboard of boat ten, supported Mr. Bradell between his knees. He did not know what time it was; he had somehow smashed his good watch. The glass was gone and the hands snapped off; there was sea water in it and some blood from Mr. Bradell's broken head. They had more than thirty Negroes on board, and this, Miro recognized, was shameful, but he could not prevent it while he had Mr. Bradell to look out for, and he told himself that if they had been the first to cut loose, he had orders to get away. Many of the other boats had been filled; one, he saw—and it frightened him more than anything else—was entirely filled with women and children. He tried to call Mr. Fenton's attention to the fact that there was no one in it capable of managing it. What would they do? Mr. Fenton paid no attention to him, and the men in number ten, mutinous at the delay, pushed off; with great difficulty got clear. Miro hoped that it might at least set the others an example; that they wouldn't wait any longer for an order to abandon. Otherwise, he understood, they might sink where they were, boats still attached, many people still on deck.

Mr. Bradell moved between his knees and Miro was seized with distress and consternation, for it occurred to him that now Mr. Bradell would realize that number ten had deliberately drawn off, leaving hundreds of people in danger of death. He said at once: "Captain's orders to abandon, sir."


Anthony's face had fallen apart, but it was bound up fairly well with a handkerchief and a hard web of pain. He did not realize anything; and not knowing how he got where he was, where he had been, nor for how long, Anthony made an effort to learn the time. The left arm with his wrist-watch he found to be no longer subject to his control. Pain of light on his eyes made him look up, and by the thin sun hung above him in the white sky he knew that it was close to noon. The boat, riding roughly, passed up a mound of water and let him see, amazed, the *San Pedro*.

He was stupefied by this sight. He had seen the *San Pedro* too often; he recognized at once that this view of her was a dream. It was impossible, it would be fatal. She could not remain like that. Here was no matter ballast-tanks could correct—her list was mortal, and at once he heard a low voice saying: *"But you do not float quite level. . . .*

He started to make a movement, to arise; and hands were instantly on him, holding him. Blood came into his mouth. A scalding void complemented his body, filling out the electric emptiness where half his face and all his shoulder should have been. Waves of heat overpowered him—so strong that with them came the imaginary smell of hot oil, the roar of the engine-room shaft. At his side, in a shabby black overcoat, he saw the horrid author of that low voice, insistent, plucking at him: *"But you do not float . . ."*

This, he knew, was entirely false; he saw, actually, nothing but the men forward, the gunwales, the mounting green water; literal things in a spinning blur of fever and pain—yet, in a way, Doctor Percival remained; the fleshless face was steady and close, brooding on them.

Seeing thus, while not seeing, he smelt stronger than salt and blood the warmed sweetness of patchouli; he was aware of the dark, despairing blue of her eyes, the

frail flippancy of her voice like a veil drawn decently over
her unspeakable desire to live.

Then, violently, without escape, he knew that this was
real, not a dream. The *San Pedro* was really there; the
ocean was in her; the sea smothered her tremendous engines. It choked up every passage and part of her;
swamped into silence the marvelous elaboration of her
machines, quenched all her lights, and would in a moment
drag her down like any broken metal. Water would do
away quickly with everything that breathed aboard her.
The boat brought him up again. Cold as he had been hot,
he saw once more the *San Pedro*.


Just adequately the *San Pedro* met each swell; no wasted
effort. She lay on her port side, down by the head, and
took her terrible rest while the mounds of water pillowed
her and washed her quietly. Like the disarray of weariness, starboard davits on the top deck dangled out trailing
ropes, suspended white boats unevenly. Expiring wisps of
steam broke in curls from her flanks. She had a screw
clear, pinned like a mighty metal flower on the slim cone
of the starboard bracket.

There she lay in a motionless lethargy, and then without pause or warning, she went. The shooting swell rose
in a hill, came quite over her bows. Her funnel inclined;
water poured freely into it, into the high hoods of her
ventilators. Deep in her, a hidden drum boom-boomed.
Like a pool, the dark gully of her promenade-deck filled
forward; steam mounted in columns through her coal-
hatches. A great metallic sigh, a six-hundred-foot shudder
—why hadn't her boilers blown, lifted thunderous through
her exhausted sides?—she was going home, going to some

deep sleep. The waters folded over her tumultuously—air, steam, the great chords booming in her hull. . . .

There remained Anthony, harassed by great pain, the boat under him, Miro behind him, the black men with the oars; if there were other boats, he could not see them. Only, overhead, the vast sky, pale and white, all around the infinite empty ocean.

# CASTAWAY

# 1 THE ASCENT INTO THE STORE

*. . . how infinitely good that Providence is, which has provided in its government of mankind such narrow bounds to his sight and knowledge of things; and though he walks in the midst of so many thousand dangers, the sight of which if discovered to him, would distract his mind and sink his spirits, he is kept serene and calm by having the events of things hid from his eyes . . .*

THE LIFE AND STRANGE SURPRIZING ADVENTURES
OF ROBINSON CRUSOE OF YORK, MARINER.

Supported against the stair rail, Mr. Lecky might have been sick; but his stomach was empty. When he retched, all that rose was a blood-warm lump—perhaps his heart bounced on the firm spurt of his terror. With this throatful, and the nausea it caused him, and the unmanageable shaking of his body, Mr. Lecky's utmost mental feat was to recognise, as finally he did, that he had reached the basement of the department store.

Panting, trying to swallow back his heart, not for a full minute could he notice what might be noteworthy: the dim, dismal illumination shed by infrequent small electric bulbs, with a world of shadows depending from pillars and massed counters; down the receding empty aisles, the subterranean silence. Since he could not see anyone, Mr. Lecky began, fearfully, to listen.

In his own head he felt as much as heard a ringing, painful and persistent, like the last of a loud detonation or stupendous jar; but Mr. Lecky was not confused. The sound that he was trying to hear would be running footsteps, the brush or bump of a quick search for him. What he would do if he heard it, Mr. Lecky did not know. In despairing anticipation he feared to hear as much as he feared not hearing anything. To be pursued and know it was hardly better than to be pursued and not know it; yet he listened. The shadowed, wanly electric-lit vast silence pressed on him as though he were sunk in a pond of quiet. Silence was so perfect that he became suddenly aware of his own breathing—hoarse regular gasps as good as signals of his whereabouts. Thinking of that, he thought too that this stillness lacked some right or natural quality. He did not believe that it was the empty quiet of desertion. Far from empty, it seemed full, as of great stealth or patiently prolonged motionlessness. Compelling his aching chest to hold in lungfuls of air as long as possible and loose them quietly, Mr. Lecky turned his congested, dreadful face from side to side. Several times not comprehending, staring with stupid furtiveness, his eyeballs sticking half paralysed on each shift, the excruciating edge of his listening unrelaxed, he beheld the long table nearest the foot of the stairs.

Its surface was covered with many shapes and sizes of kitchen knives in shining rows. Mr. Lecky continued to look at them, nipping his tongue with his teeth. Stirred then, but not with really conscious volition; not going, so

much as strongly drawn, he began to move. Four steps
took him across the aisle and he snatched a knife from the
table. The wooden hilt was set with almost a foot of broad,
never-used keen steel. Clutching it, he wheeled about, to
see who was watching him.

He could see no one. There was nothing in sight and no
more sound than before; yet his impression of something
happening, some important change in progress, had been
no illusion. The light had a different tone. The yellowish
quality of its color was being cut shade by shade; thin
shadows were in general rising movement. First distrusting
his eyes, Mr. Lecky looked directly at the bulb on the
nearest wall. Every instant the frail incandescent filaments
glowed more distinctly in their own lessening light.

Mr. Lecky sprang for the stairs. He got his left hand on
the rail. Gripping the knife to his breast, he started in a
lumbering frenzy to run up; now two, now three steps,
now stumbling, for the precipitate gloom ended sharply in
total darkness. Gaining the landing, he did not stop, but
he faltered. Pallidly down the broad opening to meet him,
he found, astonished, the gray light of dawn; and at once
his mind fabricated for him a curious reassurance. Automatic devices which turned off electric power when a certain degree of natural light reached controls somehow sensitive to it undoubtedly existed. What had made him run
was the thought of a hand stretched out to throw a switch.
Machines were something else. They knew neither hate
nor murder; they had no heads full of urgent desires or
bloody, incalculable plans. Mr. Lecky flung himself on.
At the top he glanced up and down the wide twilit aisle.
Turning sharply aside, he hid crouched against a counter
to see if anything came up after him.

Just as downstairs he had listened hard, all the while
desiring with great anguish not to hear anything, he must

wait now expectantly for what he hoped not to see. Downstairs he might not have heard; but here he would be able
to see. No one could come quietly enough to be invisible.
As seconds amounted to minutes and one minute followed
another, the pain of crouching tormented Mr. Lecky's
calves. Driven at last beyond care by it, but with his legs
now too exhausted to rise, he fell forward, thudding down
on his knees. This sound, it seemed to Mr. Lecky, must be
audible from end to end of the great main floor. He did
not look to see what came of it. Acting as though it had
not happened, he breathed on laboriously. At random he
thrust his hand into his pocket, took out his watch. It
showed quarter past five.

The information was of no value to him. Turning his
eyes aimlessly, he gazed through the glass side of the counter against which he knelt. Like all those near enough to
be seen in the growing light, it contained silverware. Side-
long, with torpid incuriosity, Mr. Lecky stared at the enclosed trifles: miniature pots and bowls for salt; shakers
for pepper; sauce boats, bonbon dishes, sweetmeat bas-
kets; tea caddies topped with colored finials; cream jugs;
engraved vinaigrettes of no special use. Looking at all
these things slowly and stupidly took some time, and suddenly Mr. Lecky grew impatient. Nothing could exceed
the folly of kneeling here, not-looking his only defence.
Still holding the knife, helped by the counter edge, he
got himself to his feet. Seeing nothing and hearing nothing, he began to walk, quickly and carefully, away from
the stair head in the silverware department, down the
broad aisle toward the outer doors.

The doors—there were ten of them set side by side in
one long heavy metal frame—were locked. Mr. Lecky's
hand was halted by an oblong of plate glass. Looking
through, he could see the spacious dusky vestibule divided

by a collapsible grill, drawn across and fastened in place. Beyond this strong steel lattice he could make out the line of doors on the street, all their narrow shades pulled down. Getting out this way would be difficult.

Mr. Lecky faced around, his back to the doors. Here, at least, he was better off. His corner commanded the cross avenues of the aisles; his back was secured. He could, of course, himself be seen from a distance, but his absolute surprise would not be easy to effect. Lifting his eyes to the source of the slowly growing light, he saw the big semi-circular window tops fifteen feet or more above a man's head. If, below the exact arc of the arch, they were real windows, the frames were covered up by woodwork descending to a point within ordinary reach. Here began multiple tiers of closed drawers.

Suppose, Mr. Lecky hazarded suddenly, he were asleep, dreaming. Dreaming, sliding into the monstrous fantasies of nightmare, he had surely felt this very breast-pressing weight of danger, made efforts to awaken, prove to himself that he was all right and nothing impended. The relief, the hope that he might open his eyes in his bed could not be accepted. He was without any doubt awake already.

Aware once more of that ringing in his ears, though it was fainter now, he tried again, his mind at work slowly. Suppose then that he had somehow injured himself and lost his memory. This was a sickness or accident of which he had often heard. People ceased to know who they were, where they came from, or even where they were going. The idea, while useful and plausible, did not satisfy him. He knew clearly that he was Mr. Lecky. He said to himself: *I remember that when I looked at my watch it was quarter past five.* Taking his watch out he looked at it and saw that he was right.

Mr. Lecky had been growing calmer, but this demonstration that he was all right, in the sense of really being where he appeared to be, and of knowing it, served to start again minute cold crispations of the skin on his shoulders. The fears he had formerly felt of hearing, and then of seeing, seemed to have changed a little. He was aware, unreasonably, of a reluctance in his perplexity, like a fear of knowing; or a resistance to it, as though he were half persuaded that what he did not know would not hurt him. Whether only in the realisation of his own mind, or in the deadly clarity of the demonstrated event—an enemy given time to catch him, or the sudden sight, the taking-in, the abrupt comprehension of something in plain sight but understood too late—an explanation was perhaps not what he wanted. Mr. Lecky looked at his knife. Though it was a large and dangerous one, he got little comfort from it.

To Mr. Lecky's left, eight elevator shafts were closed by metal doors. Half way down, affixed to the wall, he could see light reflected from a sheet of glass covering what must be the store directory. The sight of it roused him with fresh plans and improved ideas. Walking carefully, looking carefully for any sign of opposing movement, at last he turned his back on the widespread floor, began hastily to read down the long columns of white letters.

Whether he remained here, or found a means to leave, he ought certainly to possess himself of the best possible weapons. By the term Mr. Lecky understood some sort of firearm. The fact that he was totally unacquainted with the use of guns assisted him in the illusion that, given a revolver, he would instantly become formidable. Trusting machines as he did, he regarded a revolver as a small killing machine. He believed that its operation required little

more than pointing and pulling a trigger. The revolver
would obediently deliver, unerring and fast as light, death
to a great distance.

Revolvers, Mr. Lecky found at once, were not listed
here; but his reading, continuing, passed over ribbons,
rubber goods, rugs, and stopped on the words: Sporting
Goods & Outing Supplies. The generalisation gave him
immediate hope. Outing would surely mean hunting—so
important a reason for a man to deliver himself to the dis-
comforts of improvised living in the field. Hunting would
be impossible without guns.

If guns were there, they would be found on the eighth
floor, and the sooner he investigated, the better. He would,
Mr. Lecky said to himself, run right up there. Accustomed
to doing this figurative running in elevators, Mr. Lecky did
not realise to what a degree seven flights of stairs like
those he saw behind doors at the end would tax him. He
was, however, incapable of operating an elevator, even if
power to lift it were available. Looking one last time about
the main floor in the light of almost broad day, he pushed
open the pair of swinging doors. He walked to the stairs
and began to climb with impressive confidence.

One flight (no more than he was occasionally used to)
had him breathing faster, for he was in a hurry. He paused
a moment on the landing, less to recover himself than to
consider whether he ought to make an investigation of these
large floor areas he planned to pass. On the whole, he
thought, no. Until he had armed himself, the last thing he
wanted was to find anyone. He began more slowly, with
an unwelcome sense of no retreat necessarily assured, to
climb once more.

At the next landing his legs were paining him in calf
and thigh. Standing for a moment to ease them, Mr. Lecky
found his apprehensions on the increase. He did not like

the white light of the windows whose great oblongs were
sealed with a glass fused in blurring corrugations over a
wire netting. He was shut in and well enough lighted, but
he could not see out. With him he had nothing but the
kitchen knife, pushed awkwardly through his belt. No
number of weapons on the eighth floor could help him
here. Shaking himself a little, he began to climb, pausing
every step or so to hold his breath, look about him in the
blank ample light, listen, rest his legs. Thus he came to the
third landing and was confronted fairly with a weapon
better at least than a kitchen knife. Against the wall, its
handle in one bracket, its blade in a wider one, hung a
great scarlet axe. For use in case of fire, it was simply
waiting there to be taken. Mr. Lecky went and took it.

Here surely was the sort of axe they fought with in
medieval battles. More than a yard of some tough wood
formed a handle which was anchored solidly with wedges
in a steel head. It was painted scarlet, except for a narrow seven-inch arc of sharp blade edge. The other side
had been molded to a spike. No skull could stand up
against that; its point would sink easily to the core of a
man's brain. Mr. Lecky regarded the axe with appreciation, but he none the less could not help feeling its un-
handiness. To raise it and strike it against wood or a wall
might not be too difficult; to direct it at a moving opponent
was another matter—for him, probably impossible. Mr.
Lecky made a move to put it back; but even as he lifted
it he was again impressed by the long helve, the murderous head, the bright alarming color. Swung on his shoulder
it was a load, but anyone seeing him coming so equipped
might not be sure that the axe was beyond his power to
use. He began to climb once more, the helve against his
neck, the keen blade (like a gun, an axe was an instrument he had never learned to handle) at a perilous angle

behind his head. Thus, with augmented labor and straining breast, he gained the fourth floor.

Mr. Lecky's natural impulse was to sit down on the
steps a moment; but, starting to do it, he could not con-
quer an instinct to keep his face toward that approach
which would give attack the impressive advantage of im-
petus from above. Not that it would be impossible for
somebody to bound silently, far faster and more easily
than he himself had come, up from behind. He half-
wheeled merely at the thought, his back to the strip of
solid wall between the white windows; but he saw that no
such thing had happened, nor was it about to. In any
event, with luck, his axe might be effective in that direction, while in the other so useless as to make flight his
only hope. The thought of flight disquieted him, since he
had failed to arrange for a retreat. Attempting one, the
lower floor doors to the stair shaft could at any instant
swing open to cut him off. Having alarmed himself with
these possibilities and dangers, Mr. Lecky decided that it
would be better to sit down, if he must, on the half-way
landing above where the stairs doubled back on themselves. Though he was not rested and the pounding of his
unprepared heart made his stomach sick and his sight uncertain, he climbed on.

Attaining his trifling objective, Mr. Lecky was giddy.
To teach him less ambition, he seemed to taste blood in
his mouth. The axe, removed from his shoulder, was too
heavy to hold. It struck the floor of the landing with a
clash, horrible and warlike, filling the whole shaft with
the clangor of steel on steel. Supported between the unsteady helve and the rail, Mr. Lecky sank leadenly on his
buttocks, unable to make any preparations to defend himself from whatever responses might come to the still-
echoing advertisement of his presence. He rolled his head

against the thin iron posts of the rail, gulped down air jerkily. Sweat slid off all over him. Waves of hot, distinctly red-colored vibration swam across his eyes. The throb and hammer of his head excluded thought unless a despairing awareness that he was not yet much more than half way up could be called a thought.

After a long time (there was real sunlight now against the glass through which he could not see) Mr. Lecky moved again. It was, he found, overwhelmingly necessary for him to empty his bladder; and though he supposed that he might find, if he looked, some proper and decent place to do this, his exhaustion was too great for him to seek it. The act irked and disgusted him, yet he must perform it where he was. When he was done, he moved on as promptly as he could, for putting the results out of sight repaired somewhat the grossness of his impropriety. So stimulated, the excess of his effort took him to the fifth floor, and almost to the next midway landing. Here he lay in aggravated prostration for perhaps ten minutes.

Reason would suggest that after the preliminary grievous effort of getting to his feet, progress on them would be faster and easier; but when Mr. Lecky came to move again, he did not attempt to stand up. Neither did he discard the axe, which by no possible exertion could he have lifted or used. In the extremity of its exercise his will held no traffic with reason. He began, simply, step by step, to crawl, dragging the red axe with him. Thus in time he reached the sixth and seventh floors; and in more time, groaning and slobbering, the eighth. Here he lay long, defenceless, on the open landing. The worst that could come to him was death and he would not mind it. He might have fainted or slept, for with much vague time

passed, he felt somewhat stronger. In the end he was
enough restored to stand, assisted by the rail, erect.

A preliminary survey of the unknown floor which Mr.
Lecky purposed now to enter might be the part of prudence. Hardly and so newly able to stand up, Mr. Lecky
saw the uselessness of petty precautions. Though on his
feet again, the great axe still in his hand, he could
neither fight nor flee. He leaned his shoulders against the
doors, which promptly swung open, nearly letting him
fall. Staggering, he saw that he was in the toy department.


The association of ideas which accounted for the arrangement of goods in a store like this appeared reasonable, being familiar, to Mr. Lecky. The gaiety of this half acre of
playthings was even comforting. He was not dismayed. No
wagons conquering plain and mountain to jolt at last into
an Oregon ever found vaster relief or simpler joy. Mr.
Lecky stood a moment, resting again, while he examined
this goal of his.

Here among the toys, the pillars supporting the ninth
floor above had been made to look like irregular piles of
children's blocks. Mammoth, as much as a yard square,
they bore on some faces an enormous colored letter of the
alphabet, on others, an Arabic numeral, or one of the
conventionalised pictures of such everyday animals as elephants and giraffes. Around these pillars, under the additional innocent decorations of the painted walls, it was
not easy to imagine danger lurking.

Mr. Lecky walked on slowly, his axe over his shoulder,
through parks of velocipedes, tricycles, down lines of small
red-wheeled carts and sleds with light iron runners. Four
hundred square feet of table-top bore a jumble of motionless toy trains on endless circles of weak silver-colored

tracks. Beyond, another such surface supported lead sol-
diers: companies, troops, batteries, uniformed by every
nation for every war of the world's last three thousand
years. To please more practical or less imaginative children, followed counters piled with things to build or put
together: miniature airplanes, motor cars, boats, large
boxes packed with unconvincing bits of metal meant to be
structural steel.

Animals in wood and wool and rubber, of every size and
approximate shape, came next. Dolls, Mr. Lecky saw,
looking left, occupied shelves along one whole wall. However, Mr. Lecky was getting to where he wished to be, for
now appeared the various balls and sticks, the special garments and uniforms worn by children old enough to play
games in teams, needing organization. At this stage they
were, too, sufficiently inured to life to amuse themselves
in the dirt and damp of the fragmentary poor woods
and rubbish-filled coverts of nearby country-sides without
necessarily fatal results. The progression, more rapid, became one of enlarging the clothes, making heavier and
stronger the implements for play. On small platforms,
covered under foot with a shaggy green stuff representing
grass, several sorts and sizes of tents were pitched. Beside
them, colored canoes lay on bowed and swollen flanks;
small row boats turned up their light varnished planking.
Mr. Lecky walked quicker, shifting his axe to the other
shoulder. He saw frail palisades of fishing rods behind
counters whose glass-enclosed depths were strewn with
open packets of false, hook-concealing flies and gleaming
with reels. There in the corner resting, muzzles in blue
steel ranks against the green baize lining of the closed
cases, were the guns.

The cases were locked. Mr. Lecky hesitated. Then he
lowered the axe, holding it waist high in both hands. He

let it swing gently forward and the whole sheet of glass
fell to fragments at his feet. Gripping the axe, Mr. Lecky
turned in a spasm to see if that splintering crash had attracted any attention. Then he leaned the axe against the
counter behind him, reached through the door frames and
lifted out the gun at the end of the first row.

Had the question been put to him, Mr. Lecky might have
known that some difference existed between a rifle and a
shotgun; but there had never been any occasion for him to
discriminate between them. What kind of gun he held, or
what ammunition he would require, he did not know; but
he was almost satisfied merely to hold any gun in his hands.
The enormous hardship of the climb, like his judgment,
was justified. He felt already master of the whole building.

Laying down his beautiful gun, he finally set about the
search for cartridges. They were not so labelled, but the
drawers behind the counter against which his axe stood
seemed a probable place; and since they too were locked,
his axe would again be required. He was afforded small
room to swing it here, and a pointless, instinctive caution
made him at first strike gently, no more than indenting
the wood with the steel spike. When, with timorous reluctance, he hit harder, it was still a moment before he
could burst open the first drawer. Lifting it out he tipped
the contents carefully on the floor. Squatting, he examined
the heaps of clean, heavy little sealed cartons.

A simple feeling for order made Mr. Lecky soon guess
that the number with the decimal point probably referred
to size. He began to arrange the boxes in sequence of
caliber, from .22 to .303, putting aside perplexing irreg-
ularities like 25/30, 250/3000, and boxes declaring
the contents of .300 Holland & Holland magnum rimless,
or, impressively, 7.62 m/m Russian Military Bronze
Pointed. With some sixteen varieties laid out, he slit the

paper sealing on the at last useful point of his kitchen knife and prepared to try the cartridges one after another until he found those that fitted.

Mr. Lecky now encountered a difficulty at once ridiculous and formidable. Unless he were to drop these metallic cartridges down the muzzle (plainly the wrong procedure), he could find no immediate way of getting them into the gun. No doubt something ought to be pressed, turned, or pulled to give him access to the breech. He began patiently to work at every joint or projection.

Forced to observe the gun he held with care—indeed, with dawning anxiety—he saw on the barrel where it met the inflexible breech the engraved words *"Fabrique Nationale d'Armes de Guerre Herstal Belgique,"* which was plainly no direction for opening it. To Mr. Lecky these foreign words were an unpleasant discovery, suggesting a necessarily inferior weapon, and he sat still, no longer even trying to open it. He was, in fact, holding a Browning automatic twelve-gauge shotgun, complicated by magazine cutout and double extractors. For this, naturally, none of the ammunition he had laid out would serve.

Even attacked half-heartedly, the obduracy of the gun, unaffected by his pressing and pulling, soon had him sweating. It was—he began to see it some time before he could let himself admit it—hopeless. Laying the gun at last on the floor, he felt what might soon be panic. Any courage and pleasure which had first been his presupposed loading to be a trifle, quick and easy. Mr. Lecky got to his feet, hastily bringing out guns that looked in any way different and so perhaps simpler. He even produced exactly that express bolt-action sporting rifle which, had it been explained to him, he would have recognised as what he had vaguely in mind. Now, while he deduced from the small muzzle that it was more likely to take the sort of cartridges

overflowing their open boxes around him, the complexity
of the breech mechanism looked greater even than that of
the Belgian shotgun. Picking up new guns and discarding
them, Mr. Lecky worked with increasing carelessness. Em-
ploying a gun butt, he smashed the glass of the second case
and produced a staggering fresh load. Only when he had
worked over the last of these and laid it down in consternation, only when he found himself helpless amid some forty
firearms, did the idea of printed instructions occur to him.

Snatching his axe, Mr. Lecky began to break open
everything within reach that was closed. The situation
seemed too desperate for temporising, or for consideration
about quiet. He swung his exhausting axe without plan
or system, hit again and again until the drawer-fronts split
everywhere and fell to pieces. Out spilled cartridge belts,
leather and canvas gun covers, cleaning rods, swabs,
scratch brushes, flannel wipers in packages. Other drawers
soon proved to be full of special sights, telescopic mounts,
wind-gauge combinations. Sometimes more than drawers
were broken. Out issued trickles of rangoon oil, of strong-
smelling solvents for copper and nickel fouling. Crushed
and severed sections of tubes containing gun grease and
rust remover fell to the floor. Now, too, he began to find
the larger square boxes of game loads. Torn open, they
showed him red, yellow, violet, green paper shotgun shells
and he saw, distracted, that they must be meant for the
larger muzzled guns.

Turning in fury, looking for something still unbroken,
Mr. Lecky noticed on the far counter corner a heap of
small booklets. He let his axe go and, taking one in his
damp, unsteady hands, read INSTRUCTIONS FOR PURCHAS-
ERS on the cover. Exasperated to have raised such havoc
in search of something all the while in plain sight, his
fingers pressed open the pages to which they contributed

grimy smears and found for him diagrams keyed with numbers, illustrations making clear the loading and cleaning, even aiming and firing.

Mr. Lecky fell on his knees looking for weapons made by the issuer of the booklet. With one such gun across his thighs, the diagram flattened out beside him, he accomplished the simple miracle of releasing the breechbolt. Fumbling through the discovered boxes of ammunition, he filled his hands with red shells and fed them into the magazine. He closed it and locked the breech. He leaned back against the side of the counter, breathless and triumphant.

## 2  THE ARMED MAN

Armed, his energies enough restored for further action, Mr. Lecky was astonished to see by the changed direction of the light through the windows that morning had become early afternoon. This made him think of food. With immediate savage suddenness his stomach spoke to the same end. During the terrors and exertions of the long forenoon his belly must have been resigned. Except for exhaustion's occasional quakes of nausea, it had remained mute, not disturbing him while he was busy with more important matters. Now he must satisfy it. He must look for the grocery department.

Very hungry though he was, and half convinced as he
was, too, when he considered it, that the ordeal of the
stairs had been in large part due to lack of food, mere
possession of his gun put him in a more calculating frame
of mind. Sooner or later he would need, even more than
food, a place to sleep which would be as safe as he could
make it. Immediately another consideration occurred to
him. This stock of arms and ammunition ought to be safeguarded. It would be the most dangerous sort of negligence
to permit any other prowler, who might, like himself, be
originally unarmed, as easily to repair the deficiency.

Looking about him, impatient for an idea which would
free him to eat, Mr. Lecky's eye fell on a group of fitting-
rooms in the section devoted to sports clothing. This structure consisted of six closet-like compartments where cus-
tomers might retire to try on the garments hanging ready
for them in the nearby cases. Although it stood perhaps a
yard higher than a man's head, Mr. Lecky could see
through an open door that it was not roofed over. Presented
with this concrete problem, he thought at once of knocking out the hinge pins from the doors. Doors would do very
well, once loose and at his disposal, for making a platform
on top. By moving thither his guns and cartridges, and
what food he might need, he would have a citadel, if not
impregnable, at least fairly commanding and proof against
surprise.

Pleased by his plan, he could even consider a moment
the advisability of making the arrangements at once. He
decided not to. His present hunger and weakness might
make the task of removing and raising the doors and
carrying all the guns beyond his strength.

Amid the surrounding wreckage Mr. Lecky noticed and
now picked up a belt of webbing fitted with numerous

narrow loops to hold shotgun shells. Strapping it around his waist he filled the more accessible openings with the proper ammunition. Taking up the gun, which he held alertly in both hands, he went the shorter distance to the elevators on this side. From the directory posted there he learned that groceries were on the sixth floor; and cheered by this relative nearness, he pushed open the swinging doors with his foot. Into the stair shaft he came cautiously, gun, muzzle first, finger on the trigger. Seeing and hearing nothing, he began his descent, quiet, watchful, but almost sick with hunger.

By gracious accident, Mr. Lecky had picked the side and the stairs which, on the sixth floor, allowed him to step directly into the grocery department. He did not have to pass through the great reaches displaying glass and china which adjoined it. His mouth, as the general faint odor of so much food reached him, was suddenly swimming with saliva. His head swam, too; and, incautiously setting the butt of his loaded gun on the floor, he supported himself a moment by leaning on the muzzle while the ordered tables swung across his eyes.

Most immediately at hand was one side of a bright pyramid of shelves surrounding a pillar. They were entirely filled, he saw, amazed, with sardines. In jars, with olive oil, with lemon, with truffles; French fish in tins; Bordelaise; boneless and skinless Portuguese packings; smoked Norwegian Bristling; sardines in wine sauce, in every shape of tin and glass. Some of these Mr. Lecky could get at quickly since the flat tins were equipped with keys to tear off and roll back the metal tops. He began to snatch them up while he moved in a nervous anguish of greed, disclosing to

himself the pyramid's right side. This was black with caviar
in glass of descending sizes. Against this side Mr. Lecky
rested his gun. Applying a key to a sardine tin, he wrenched
back the top, spilling the olive oil in his shaking hands. He
dug in with his fingers and greedily filled his mouth with
half a handful of broken fish.

The taste of food restored Mr. Lecky from the witless-
ness of his first snatching. The tin was empty and he put it
aside on a table edge. Deliberately he filled his pockets
with more tins; for, should he be interrupted, or by some
chance find nothing easier to get at, he could always have
sardines. Taking up his gun again, he wiped his hand on
his trousers and moved on, jaws still busy with his great
mouthful.

Perhaps he had been wise to fill his pockets with sardines. All the adjacent displays were of vegetables in glass
jars: hills of visible, chill and sodden small beets; thin
beans, white or too green; peas poisonously bright, and
yellow messes of corn. Eventually these might be valuable,
in view of that part of Mr. Lecky's convictions having to do
with physiology and health. He believed that it was necessary to include vegetables in his diet, but now he had no
time for them.

He had reached biscuits and packaged cakes; and Mr.
Lecky gathered up some of the smaller and more convenient boxes. His gun was again a nuisance. He set it down to
tear open a package and refill his mouth. Busy with this,
he saw through an arch beyond a whole ceiling hung with
smoked and wrapped hams. At once he dropped the remaining biscuits. Forgetting his gun, he hastened to possess
himself of what he considered proper, solid food. Jerking
down a ham, described on its wrapper as cooked, he
realised that what he needed now was the kitchen knife,

left where he had used it to open the cartridge boxes upstairs. Immediately he remembered, too, his gun; and
clutching his prize, he rushed back to get that.

Mr. Lecky would not very soon forget his sensation when
he rounded the first of the biscuit counters and found that
his gun was not there. He dropped his desirable ham on
the floor, frozen in terror too exquisite for any phrase or
adequate thought. His hair actually lifted on his head.
There was not a sound, nor any visible movement. The
gun was simply gone.

He took an undirected step, and another, chiefly to keep
his balance, for he did not know which way to flee, nor
what to flee from. Doing this, he discovered, almost faint-
ing in reaction, that his gun was exactly where he had left
it, behind the second table.

With the blue metal in his icy hands, he stood shaking.
He felt that death had brushed by him. He was not
wholly certain of the miss. He turned, still trembling, finding the floor in front higher at every step than his foot expected. His fingers hooked on the counter edge, he stooped
and picked up the ham. In the same uncertain way he
selected a large tin box of biscuits. Carrying both, and
the gun, he walked, shocked and stupid, to the doors by
which he had entered.

This load was much clumsier than the axe, but sense of
a direction already determined, perhaps the few mouth-
fuls of food which he had thrown his stomach, made it
possible for him to climb in his diminishing numbness
steadily and quickly. Prying open the door on the eighth
floor, he pushed through, ham and biscuit box insecurely
against his breast, gun swinging in his aching fingers. The
unchanged silence awaited him. Proceeding to the counter

where his knife rested, he set down box and ham, propped the gun against his thigh. Ripping the cloth package from around the meat and slashing off the stubborn thick rind at the end, Mr. Lecky cut himself a slab of ham perhaps an inch through. Sparing his right hand now to hold the gun, he sank his teeth into this formidable slice.

His hunger finally satisfied, Mr. Lecky looked for water. A white porcelain drinking fountain of the sort which, at pressure on a button, threw up a jet, came promptly to his eye. It stood by the stair doors. As he went toward it he realised that there might be no water in it, or in whatever pipes or tanks fed it. Foreseeing the annoyance of a second trip to the sixth floor for some kind of bottled beverage, he was surprised when the button, pressed, produced the right result. Water leaped freely up and he captured it in his mouth. Fresher now, by contrast, rested, he returned to the cases of firearms and reconsidered his idea for spending the night.

This still seemed perfectly practicable. The first move would be to take off the doors and cover the open compartments with them. Whether the removal could be managed with his bare hands was the one doubtful point. If tools were needed, certainly he could hope to find none nearer than the basement. Tomorrow it might be wise to undertake such an expedition and add a hammer, pliers, a screw driver, to his equipment. Meanwhile he had his axe with which he could probably break the doors from their hinges.

So thinking, absorbed in calculation, he noticed an object fallen from one of the split drawers. It was a loading tool for metallic cartridges, but to Mr. Lecky it looked very much like an unhandy but strong pair of complicated pliers.

Taking it, and being careful to bring his gun with him this time, he went over to the fitting-rooms. He applied his supposed pliers to the round head of the hinge pin, managed to manipulate the handles until they held. He jerked. To his great pleasure, the pin gave promptly, lifted out and fell to the floor. The door sagged off, hanging only by the upper hinge.

A chair from inside the compartment now enabled Mr. Lecky to reach and remove this hindrance. Free, the door leaned, and he steadied it while he dismounted. Seeing that his gun was as conveniently close as it could be, Mr. Lecky took the door in both hands, raised it against the upper edge of the compartment wall. Pushing and heaving, he got the door up until it half rested, almost balancing. Hopping and shoving, he moved it further and further until, releasing it cautiously, he found that it had reached, landing with a light thud, the other side. There it was.

This operation had proved encouragingly easy, in the sense that he had been able to do it at all; but the necessary incidental exertion made him decide, when he had laboriously put them up, that three doors would be enough. The afternoon was drawing on, and the task of transporting the guns and getting himself settled on his citadel would be no work of a moment. Considering the last point, he saw that he ought to provide something soft for him to sit or lie on, since he would be obliged to do one or the other for many hours—a few heaps of the clothes in the nearby cases would serve. Sliding back the glass door of the nearest case, he helped himself to coats—short, but thickly lined with matted fleece. Having thrown out a considerable pile on the floor, he gathered up an armful. Getting precariously on the chair, he succeeded in lifting and clumsily tossing this collection across the horizontal doors. No more than two or three went too far and fell off the other side. Another armful would do no harm, he decided.

His ham and his box of biscuits could go up next. He could also relieve himself of the sardine tins which had been bulging his pockets uncomfortably. There remained the arms and ammunition.

So many guns would leave no room for himself, and Mr. Lecky had a helpful inspiration. Anyone who needed a gun would need ammunition, too. If he brought over all the cartridges, he could bring only a few guns, to which at leisure, he might fit the proper shells, so if the worst came to some unpredictable worst, he would be spared the helpless pause of reloading.

Time was growing valuable. His watch, he found, had stopped. It still declared quarter past five, and could, indeed, have been correct again; but held to his ear, it made no sound. He might as well assume that quarter past five was the time, wind it, and let it proceed on that basis. When he had done this he went about collecting and carrying over the ammunition. There was a great deal of it, so he spent surely no less than half an hour; but when he had finished and selected his guns, and was ready to get up himself, his watch still said quarter past five. Plainly it was broken and useless. He returned it to his pocket, disgruntled.

By assembling three chairs, seats together in a circle, it was possible to place on them two chairs, facing each other. A little caution in movement would let him climb them. The chairs remained, convenient for someone else to use, but he could no doubt knock them down from above. Mr. Lecky saw no other way at all of effecting an ascent. He was not young enough, and far from athletic enough, simply to lay hold on the high edge, raise himself until he could swing a leg over one of the compartment tops still left open and rise easily erect, straddling the wall.

He could, however, imagine an active enemy doing it. The best safeguard he could think of would be a row of small objects, almost any kind, distributed along the edges. Anyone attempting that approach while Mr. Lecky slept could hardly help knocking off some of these small things and so warning him. Frowning, he took his gun and went in among the toys.

A short search revealed nothing so convenient and so certain to cause a great racket falling as the light metal cars forming the toy trains. Detaching half a dozen of them from their locomotives, he brought them back. Taking down one of his chairs to stand on, he set these toys at intervals on the compartment edges not covered by his three doors. Returning the chair to its previous position, he climbed up.

Once on top amid the unarranged accumulation of his miscellaneous gear, Mr. Lecky found that six doors would have been much better than three. He crouched, in effect, on a little raft whose instability was increased by the careless, uneven placing of what doors he had. The ends of two of them protruded into space, where also they were ready to tilt him and his supplies if any movement of his shifted the center of gravity too far. This he corrected as well as he could, painstakingly moving the heaps of clothes and cartridges and food to leave one after another of the doors clear. Squatting down on the other two, he could then tug the free one into a more secure and orderly position. The double pile of coats he arranged in a low rampart, sorry now that he did not have more. Whatever the actual strength, a wall, even low and of cloth, gave an illusion of shelter. On it the guns could be laid, pointed in various directions, ammunition stacked to one side.

Mr. Lecky had been so absorbed in these adjustments that the stealthy growth of shadows into a general gloom became only now inescapably apparent. Lifting his head he saw it, and with consternation. His one serious, almost incredibly heedless oversight was demonstrated. All day long he had neglected the matter of lights. The dark coming down was already rendering useless both his eyes and his guns.

The recognition of his carelessness filled Mr. Lecky with fear and anger. In the dusk his eerie heart could anticipate the hours of terror which he had laid up for himself. Sounds, real or imaginary, the silences and secrets of the night, the working of his own mind, skilled in cruel illusion and rich in evil fancy, would find him without recourse.

Here was nothing sitting still could cure, and cured, it seemed to him, it must be. Perhaps, had he not known that electric torches were sure to be available somewhere, Mr. Lecky might have found the mental means to survive without them. Natural resources of brain and nervous system could and would adapt themselves to the inevitable; but they made no compromise with convenience. Only in the last uncontrollable stage did they make one with exhaustion.

If fear, unconscionable, bade Mr. Lecky be up, common sense bade him be quick, undertake his descent into the store while some light remained to help him. He bound on the web belt full of shells. He advanced the loaded shotgun to the edge so that he might reach up and get it from the floor. Then he let himself down.

The stairs were lighter. A pale lucid twilight lay on the steps and landings to hearten Mr. Lecky a little, but very little. Although resigned to the proposition that a light was necessary, and so concentrated on the means to make a light, although harassed by the importance of haste, and the hope of being back soon at his safe base, Mr. Lecky moved reluctantly. He was wearier in bone and muscle than he felt. He went heavily, even thoughtlessly, for he had descended a flight of stairs before he recalled that he had never troubled to learn, from the directory, where he was going.

He was both discouraged and frightened while he halted at the doors of the seventh floor. The unknown reaches which they hid would be dark; he might not even be able to read the directory. Wasting thus moments which he could not afford, he peered finally into the squares of glass set at the level of his face, pushed irresolutely, holding his gun tight, and stepped through. The darkness was not so deep as he had imagined that it would be. He could still see that this part of the floor held heaps of rugs, rolls of carpet. Moving along the elevators, the goods changed to draped upholstery fabrics, dim piles of pillows, rows of false windows set up to display the uses of curtain materials. He could not tell what might be hiding among them, so he did not try. Instead, staring closely at the dim white lines of the directory, straining his eyes, his nose almost against the glass, he learned that flashlights were on the main floor.

Insentient matter, putting itself wantonly as far from him as possible, could not be commanded to come; and if he cursed it, it could not hear or fear him. Slowly, disheartened beyond precaution, Mr. Lecky went out again, on down, not thinking any more than he could help of the climb back.

Arrived finally on the main floor, he found here light almost as good as that dying in the stair shaft. He found too that what he sought was close to the stairs, in counters im-

mediately fronting the rank of useless elevators. He tried
to take heart, for with flashlights he was more familiar
than with guns. He could select at once two electric lanterns—squat rectangular cases of olive-green metal whose
batteries would not be used up even should they burn for
hours. To these he added a long torch. By the size of the
bulb, reflector, and magnifying lens, it promised him a
powerful hundred-foot shaft. These three would serve very
well. He checked them for batteries, bulbs and their proper
functioning. Pushing his gun under his arm, hanging the
lanterns by the clasps on their back to his cartridge belt,
and holding the long torch in his hand, Mr. Lecky turned
back to the stairs.

Since he had light, he snapped it on. One of the weighty
lanterns sagging at his belt, tilted forward, threw a pool of
radiance shaking and swaying on the steps as it jerked and
bobbed to his climbing. This was good, and good too was
the knowledge that he had somewhere to go; but he knew
it vaguely only, in an apathy of exhaustion which saw good
things after all not very different from bad. So he began
the great labor of the climb back to the eighth floor and
the security of his citadel.

Mr. Lecky never got any farther than the third floor.
Not conscious of impossible fatigue, feeling less than his
distress of the morning, he was notwithstanding seized by a
faintness. This sudden spinning dizzied him. A darkness as
impalpable, more discrete, yet blacker than night's, spun
out from dancing points to overlapping disks. They were
so wide, so close to his eyes, that he could not strike them
off. He had only a second given him to see and apprehend.
This same second loosened his grip on consciousness. He
seemed to let go, hardly struggling. His muscles let go
everywhere, too. He had time to hear, like some remote
accident, the bang of the shotgun, gone the smash of glass

in at least one flashlight lens. This was the thin segment
of the actual second, and Mr. Lecky knew nothing of himself slumping to lie on the stairs with the things he had
dropped.

## 3 THE FORTIFICATION OF THE
LAVATORY

Following its outraged failure, Mr. Lecky's body, though
unused to sleeping on steel, made no effective protest. Its
discomfort could not penetrate the stupor enwrapping him.
At most there was a twitching of muscles, the gradual performance of movements which completed his slipping,
carrying him to a more satisfactory rest on the level landing. He had lain without concern for ten hours when
strengthening light on the fused glass aroused him. His eyes
opened.

Reduced temperature and cramped circulation squeezed
pain from all his joints as Mr. Lecky tried to move. Without, that instant, knowing where he was, he knew at least
that he should not be there. Drowsily knowing that, he was
jolted completely awake. The information, the memory
and the apprehension he might need for safety or self-
defence were given him in one burst. His heart swelled
with the blood to nourish thought or flight; his sore muscles
tightened excruciatingly in case he cared to spring away.
Only his eyelids were slow, stuck together at the corners,

and he rubbed them while he looked, gasping, for his gun.
Seeing it, Mr. Lecky with great pain sat up. Although
he was almost crippled by his stiffness he pulled the gun
down from the step above.

It was the quickest, best medicine for his natural fright.
Faith, said to have moved mountains, entered Mr. Lecky
in force as he saw himself safely re-equipped to kill. He
leaned against the rail, tottering, grunting, as each new
sinew was drawn and flexed dolorously. At the same time
his ears reported the perfect stillness, his eyes in rapid
movement found nothing to mark but the flashlights he
had dropped. He looked at his watch then, discovering,
even as he remembered its uselessness, that it still showed
quarter past five.

Now he was concerned about his other property: the
flashlights—whether they had been damaged. Moving with
a preliminary awkwardness, he saw the remains of a lens
in pieces on the steps. He held the gun under his elbow
and pressed the thumb switches on the others. In both cases
he got, satisfied, immediate useless winks of pale yellow
light. Even the broken one he might find parts for, so he attached it to his belt again, not reflecting that where these
had been found were many more. Only the batteries were
actually important to him, or might in time come to be.

Mr. Lecky was next aware of hunger. This tyranny astonished him. Feeding himself all his life at needlessly
frequent, conventional hours, appetite had been to him
hardly more than a desirable adjunct to the formalities of
sitting down and waiting for food to be brought. So casual
an act did not seem to have any important relation to himself as a living creature. Yesterday, fear and weariness, reliable exterminators of abstract thought, withheld the novel
lesson. Today, Mr. Lecky could not miss this aspect of
himself. To think that he was a contrivance which must be

filled with breakfast in order to operate amused him; the trifling light-headedness of hunger made him laugh. Food, the ham and biscuits, he had upstairs; and remembering them, he must remember his hard labor to make himself a refuge which in the end he had not used. This, too, amused him.

He began to climb, the gun grasped about the lock in one hand. He had gained the sixth floor, with two pauses only, before the impatience of his stomach reminded him that he need not eat up frugally what he already had. Food, all his, was right here in quantities to be measured by the ton.

Putting his face toward the sixth-floor doors, a certain wariness returned to him. Mr. Lecky stopped long enough to shift his gun into a position of readiness; but, stepping through, he allowed himself to be quickly reassured. He advanced with the confidence of proprietorship into the grocery department.

By long habit he ate fruit for breakfast. Somewhere there might be fruit in its natural state, but since he saw first preserved figs in a glass jar, it seemed to him simpler to eat those. He tucked his gun under his arm again and made a moment's attempt with his thumbs to break the seal of the vacuum cap. Finding the effort futile, and having no opener to give him a little leverage under the pounds of thin air which pressed it in place, he was presently moved to try the effect of striking the slightly narrowed mouth against the counter edge.

Mr. Lecky had meant only to knock the cover off; but his sharp blow was inaccurate. The neck smashed, strewing glass splinters, syrup, and a few of the figs in a mess on counter and floor. Mr. Lecky was annoyed. Furthermore, he feared that bits of glass might have embedded themselves in the remaining fruit. Setting down his gun, he made a meticulous examination, for he believed that swallowed glass would surely kill him. Partly satisfied that he was not about to eat any, he began to pick the figs out, cautiously looking over each before thrusting it in his mouth. Once or twice the grating of the fine seeds on his teeth made him pause; but hunger urged him on. Setting down the empty bottle, he could think of nothing to fetch and eat next but a second ham.

His knife was again left upstairs, he discovered. He must use his fingers. Not meant for claws, they would not serve Mr. Lecky for them. He was reduced finally to gnawing; but since he lacked the efficient incisors of proper carnivora, and his molars were flat instead of pointed, that was not easy either. He had lost his taste for ham, now that his jaws were weary and his mouth coated with the expressed oil of pig fat. Giving up, he contented himself with biscuits and water from a drinking fountain. That would do for the moment; and done, he had occasion to think of matters after all related. He must find a lavatory.

The quest took him hastily down the side of the long floor until he discovered what he sought—a door on the far side by the stairs opposite those which he had heretofore used. Closeting himself and attaining relief, Mr. Lecky had leisure to meditate, partly at least in terms of the fittings and furnishings around him. Any permanent quarters would have to be planned to include these facilities.

*We imagine much more fitly an artificer upon his close stool or on his wife than a great judge, reverend for his carriage and regardful for his sufficiency.*

Mr. Lecky, emerging at last from his retirement stood thoughtful, with his shotgun, considering by what means he could make habitable and fortify a lavatory.

To the problem of his defence, Mr. Lecky brought a conventional imagination. The first step would be to surround
himself with a wall or barricade. This would both conceal
and protect him, and halt or considerably impede any attack. Nothing would so well serve this purpose as solid
pieces of furniture. The furniture department would be
full of them.

Mr. Lecky went at once to consult the directory and
then by the most convenient stairs to the ninth floor, his
mind active on the enlargement and improvement of his
idea. As he had expected, the lavatories were placed one
above another from floor to floor; and, standing by the
lavatory door, he marked out with his eye the lines of his
projected enclosure. To form it at all he would first have to
move a number of heavily upholstered chairs. Pushing
one chair until it bumped another, in turn bumping another, he was able to get whole rows into slow motion.

Pieces of furniture such as he had planned to use—bureau bookcases, drop-front secretaries, cabinet desks—
were not conveniently placed for the purpose. He must
resign himself to moving them, toil likely to be notable
when only the heavier and more substantial pieces would
be the ones he wanted. Reflection brought him to reduce
the scale of his plan. Five pieces to a side might be
enough.

Mr. Lecky took off his coat, dropped it in a chair and
laid his gun on it. That much less encumbered, he walked
down among the beds. Here he picked out a cot furnished
not only with springs, but with a sample mattress. Pulling
it from its position, controlling its persistent side-move-
ments, he got it easily enough roundabout through the
wider aisles until it stood close to his lavatory door. Immediately he left it, and the chair where lay his coat under
the gun, to select the pieces for his fort walls.

Moving the desks was hard work and it did not take Mr.
Lecky long to decide that a semi-circle would be a better
shape for his fort than a square. It would spare him three
or four trips, and if he were glad to escape extra exertion,
he also shrank from prolonging in any way the noise he
had to make. His heavy pieces in progress destroyed the
silence with a rumbling scrape and a squeak. Some of
them made sounds not impossible for a human throat to
form. Some others seemed to simulate dragging footsteps.
All of them, crossing certain, probably hollow, parts of the
floor, made a noise like muttering thunder or far-off ex-
plosions.

At first completely occupied, and content as every
man occupied completely is, Mr. Lecky, thinking how far
this bang and rumble must carry, grew less content. He
broke off his work frequently, restoring the silence to listen. He looked often at the stair doors near—too near—
his incomplete fort. The doors hung closed and motionless. Through their panes of glass, face-high, nothing
watched him; but, just as the next noise he made might be
covering some sound, the instant after he looked away
some countenance might rise to the empty square of glass.
Like recurring cold on his sweaty face, the bad feeling that
he was perhaps no longer alone kept coming and going
slowly. Hesitating, his hands against the desk he had been
pushing, Mr. Lecky was unable to support this doubt. He
moved suddenly, ferociously agile, bounding toward the
chair with his coat and gun.

The gun was still good tonic. Compact, hard, and real,
it gave him a reassurance born of touch; his nerves steadied to the solid smooth stock and the long perfect steel
barrel. There had been no sound when he moved; there
was none now while he held the gun; and then, gradually,
the sense of being secretly watched grew less and ceased.

Mr. Lecky went back to his work. He took his gun with him this time, resolved not to be so far from it again; but his confidence had returned. His conscious mind believed or wished to believe that what had been no more than vaguely felt, and now was felt no more, must never have existed outside his imagination. Unconsciously, since he wanted the gun with him, notwithstanding, he could not have been blind to the other chance—a different, perhaps dreadful, good reason for feeling alone, unwatched again.

Laid on top of whatever piece engaged him, the gun went back and forth with Mr. Lecky, and so he finished his task. Leaving the last desk at an angle, he stepped into the shadows of his fort, climbed onto the table with which he had provided himself and looked over his strange rampart. He stood for some time, his elbows on a cabinet top, looking in silence. After a while he noticed that he was again hungry, and, judging it to be noon, got down. This time it would be easier to go to the eighth floor and bring up the provisions he had put there last night. He could eat, rest a little, and then move the arms and ammunition. Afterwards he must get rope to bind the pieces of his barricade into position.

When he had entered the eighth floor and crossed it, Mr. Lecky was not greatly impressed, except by their disadvantages, to see the measures he had taken for his security yesterday. He recovered his ham, beside which he saw the knife he had that morning needed. Sawing off a chunk of meat and taking a handful of biscuits, he ate both standing, anxious to complete his work.

Four guns made load enough to climb with. As for the ammunition, a knapsack or pack basket, both available among the outing equipment, would enable him to transport considerable quantities at a time. Moving to where the pitched tents stood on their platforms and mats of artificial grass, Mr. Lecky found what he wanted.

When he had made four trips, heavily laden, he rested again, ate another slice of ham, and retired to his lavatory to drink from a faucet. Refreshed, he could now consider today's trip into the store.

The pack basket on his back, the shotgun, his left hand closed over the breech and lock plates, swinging muzzle-first at his side, Mr. Lecky descended the stairs not without caution. It was however the caution of a man who guards prudently against the disadvantage of surprise, not that of one who expects an encounter to cost him his life.

This was well enough in the stair shaft full of diluted afternoon sunlight; but the vast main floor, so high, so open, was already shadowed. The mouths of the basement stairways seemed to be emitting a little of the abundance of darkness below. The silent sunless air was tinged with a chill gloom through which the spaced great pillars closed up in perspective. From Mr. Lecky's point of entrance, they fell into line across the floor. As Mr. Lecky advanced, they changed first into confusion, then, at a certain point, into new lines drawn diagonally from corner to corner. When he reached the head of the stairs near the silver-ware department, they had moved again. In new departure, they were aligned from end to end.

This ordinary phenomenon of perspective was given extravagant attention, for Mr. Lecky found himself absorbed, in a way, stupefied, by the mighty effort his reason was making to keep him from being afraid. His tongue busied itself constantly with his dry lips. He breathed deeply, pushing air to the bottom of his lungs. He looked about him tentatively, up and down, once or twice sharply over his shoulder, but to no purpose. He saw and questioned details—the intricate metal nipples of a sprinkler system for fire control at regular intervals on the high ceiling; down the aisles and counters, the department numbers, the small glass and bronze signs naming the goods sold under them. He could see the silverware behind the glass of its counter fronts; he looked searchingly at the small empty information booth, down at the floor, up at the pillars. Some had the gratings of ventilators set in them. To one by the stairs was affixed the round gong, the perforated, square magnet and coil box of a big electric bell.

Mr. Lecky could not be overlooking anything, and all things were in order, and none of them needed his attention; but he found himself yawning—a spasmodic, involuntary gulp-in of the tasteless air which had nothing to do with drowsiness. Powerless to account for or to control this deep apprehension, he no longer wanted to enter the basement, nor even to remain here near the stairs. Foreboding oppressed him; yet, yawning again, shaking himself a little, he looked about, not ready to be driven away, reviewing futilely the high sprinkler valves, the ventilating grills, the information booth, the silver in the counters, the big electric bell on the pillar.

Rope, he remembered, was what he had come for. He needed it to bind together his fort upstairs. There might not be any rope in the basement, and with a sort of joy, he thought how well, how much better, leather belts would be. These he could probably find on this floor, and knowing that it was no longer necessary to go downstairs, he began to wonder if he ought not to go a little way down, flash a light around and show himself that nothing was there.

Walking over and leaning across the counter whose sliding back he had last night left open, Mr. Lecky picked out one of the long-shafted torches, tried the switch with his thumb. He laid it beside his gun. He freed his shoulders from the packstraps and set the basket down. Taking his weapon in his right hand and the light in his left, he went directly to the wide stair entrance. Snapping on the light, he pointed it to strike straight and far in front of him over the descending rails and onto the open counters of the basement.

It gave him, as such play of light and shadow can, an instant's bad shock, for he thought he saw something crouched or lying on the basement floor at the foot of the stairs. The shaft of light leaped and shook, showed him the great variety of shadows and the mistakes he could make about him; but he was on the half-way landing, and he stopped, half satisfied, and that was enough. Turning the shaft of light in an aimless wide circle, he turned, too.

He was shaking now. The instant's halt released his joints and muscles, making him shake freely. The trembling paralysed him. Attempting to get his body again under his direction, it seemed to resist, meaning never to serve him, never to let him get up. Then, at once, it yielded; the muscles drew, the joints articulated.

His shoes, lifting with a scrape from step to step, seemed to Mr. Lecky to echo inordinately. It was a double sound, not unlike someone following him. The insistent, the insane realness of this impression, was hard to bear, and yet Mr. Lecky had no faith in it. Since he had not, courage, or his feeble assertion of courage, forbade him to perform the two natural acts—turning to see or hurrying.

At the top he faced about, jerking stiffly, and saw the staircase empty. In the relaxation of his nerves—some tense still, some eased, and so himself figuratively awry— he was exhilarated with the demonstration of such a triumph over nothing. He could even walk arrogantly through the counters searching for belts. Let anyone beware; Mr. Lecky was coming.

Finding them, he counted out the number he would need and returned. There remained nothing for Mr. Lecky to do but collect as many lanterns as he could. When he had loaded the basket, he squatted, got his arms through the straps and came erect, the pack falling into place. He departed then, pushing his way through the stair-shaft doors. His load was not light and he had a long way to go.

Resting, as he did six separate times, Mr. Lecky occupied himself with the thought of further things he might use and could get tomorrow. The measure was in a way defensive. With dusk gathering even in the stair shaft, he was suffering again that illusion of the double sound. An echo, properly his, confused itself with some blurred undertone, as of parallel movement, stopping when he stopped, moving when he moved again. On the fifth floor the illusion was so compelling that Mr. Lecky leaned on the rail and, dragging a flashlight awkwardly out, directed its light down the central void. He saw nothing except the floor far under him, the exact lines of the invariable diagonally-sinking stair rails, one below another.

At last—it was darker than dusk now and he used a light—he attained the ninth floor, made his way wearily but without trouble to his silent fort. Once inside he pulled into place the desk he had left at an angle for an entrance. The pack he let down on the narrow mattress of his cot, and he sat beside it. His confidence or relief was less than he had expected. The lights to which he was ordinarily accustomed were violent, spendthrift floods. Even as many as four of these lanterns, all on together, served chiefly to show him how heavy and jealous was the outer darkness.

# 4 THE CREATURE FEEDING

When he had eaten, Mr. Lecky lay down on his cot, though he did not expect to sleep. The four lanterns continued to shed their thin floods of light. Against the dark, this illumination set the varied, ill-matched shapes of his assembled defences. Studying the odd wall, in spirit unquiet, Mr. Lecky was reminded of his childhood—not in any detail of actual reminiscence, but more deeply, less coherently. He seemed to recall himself, unreally small and young, in concealment under a table. A table had been fort enough, for his enemies were imaginary. He never imagined them winning.

Even at that early period, furniture would only be useful against foes which he had invented to play with. Tables could not have protected him from bears or wolves. Perhaps he had been taught, by his amused elders, a conventional fear of bears. Unassisted, he had picked up a private fear of wolves. Bears were no more than vague monsters coming at night, never distinct nor well defined. But of wolves his unruly imagination could produce whole lifelike packs such as those which he had somehow been led to believe pursued any sleigh venturing out, three frantic horses abreast, in perpetually snow-sunk Russia.

At a brief later stage he had entertained, fruit of the new-found ability to read, some concern about ghosts. His spectres were, however, practically people, if hideous, gaunt and pale ones. It was doubtful if he ever actually believed in them, in the sense of fearing that he might meet one. His eyesight had always been good, so it played him none of the terrifying tricks necessary to confirm a belief in the supernatural. Indeed, he could not be long in discovering that people beyond a suspicion of unbalance, or not obviously coveting the moment's arrest of attention gained them by their statements, never had experience with or knowledge of the restless dead. Slowly accepting this as evidence that no such things existed, Mr. Lecky found terrors deeper, and to him more plausible, to fill that unoccupied place—the simple sense of himself alone, and, not unassociated with it, the conception of a homicidal maniac quietly pursuing him.

The first was exemplified by chance solitude in what he had considered deep woods. No part in it was played by natural dismay which he might have felt at finding himself lost, and none by any tangible suggestion of danger. Mr. Lecky could not even remember where or when it was. Long ago, under a seamless gray sky which would probably end with snow; in an autumnal silence free from birds, unmoved by the least breath of wind, he had come to be walking at random impulse.

Leaves, yellow, tan, drifted deep and loose over the difficulties of an uneven hillside. His feet crashed and crackled in them. He was not going anywhere. He had nothing in mind. It might have been this receptive vacancy of thought which let him, little by little, grow aware of a menace. The unnatural light leaf-buried ground, the low dark sky, the solitary noise of his unskilled progress—none of them was good. He began to notice that though the fall of leaves left an apparent bright openness, in reality it merely pushed to a distance the point at which the woods became as impenetrable as a wall.

He walked more and more slowly, listening, hearing

nothing; looking, seeing nothing. Soon he stopped, for he was not going any farther. Standing in the deep leaves beneath trees bare and practically dead in the catalepsy of impending winter, he knew that he did not want to be here. A great evil—no more to be named than, met, to be escaped—waited fairly close. So he left. He got out of those woods onto an open road where he need not watch for anything he could not see.

About his madmen Mr. Lecky was no more certain. He knew less than the little to be learned of the causes or even of the results of madness. Yet for practical purposes one can imagine all that is necessary. As long as maniacs walk like men, you must come close to them to penetrate so excellent a disguise. Once close, you have joined the true werewolf.

Pick for your companion a manic-depressive, afflicted by any of the various degrees of mania—chronic, acute, delirious. Usually more man than wolf, he will be instructive. His disorder lies in the very process of his thinking, rather than in the content of his thought. He cannot wait a minute for the satisfaction of his fleeting desires or the fulfillment of his innumerable schemes. Nor can he, for two minutes, be certain of his intention or constant in any plan or agreement. Presently you may hear his failing made manifest in the crazy concatenation of his thinking aloud, which psychiatrists call "flight of ideas." Exhausted suddenly by this riotous expense of speech and spirit, he may subside in an apathy dangerous and morose, which you will be well advised not to disturb.

Let the man you meet be, instead, a paretic. He has taken a secret departure from your world. He dwells amidst choicest, most dispendious superlatives. In his arm he has the strength to lift ten elephants. He is already two hundred years old. He is more than nine feet high; his chest is of iron, his right leg is silver, his incomparable head is one whole ruby. Husband of a thousand wives, he has begotten on them ten thousand children. Nothing is mean about him; his urine is white wine; his faeces are always soft gold. However, despite his splendor and his extraordinary attainments, he cannot successfully pronounce the words: electricity, Methodist Episcopal, organisation, third cavalry brigade. Avoid them. Infuriated by your demonstration of any accomplishment not his, he may suddenly kill you.

Now choose for your friend a paranoiac, and beware of the wolf! His back is to the wall, his implacable enemies are crowding on him. He gets no rest. He finds no starting hole to hide him. Ten times oftener than the Apostle, he has been, through the violence of the unswerving malice which pursues him, in perils of waters, in perils of robbers, in perils of his own countrymen, in perils by the heathen, in perils in the city, in perils in the wilderness, in perils in the sea, in perils among false brethren, in weariness and painfulness, in watchings often, in hunger and thirst, in fastings often, in cold and nakedness. Now that, face to face with him, you simulate innocence and come within his reach, what pity can you expect? You showed him none; he will certainly not show you any.

*Lighten our darkness, we beseech thee, O Lord; and by thy great mercy defend us from all the perils and dangers of this night; for the love of thy only Son, our Saviour, Jesus Christ. Amen.*

Mr. Lecky's maniacs lay in wait to slash a man's head half off, to perform some erotic atrocity of disembowelment on a woman. Here, they fed thoughtlessly on human flesh; there, wishing to play with him, they plucked the mangled Tybalt from his shroud. The beastly cunning of their approach, the fantastic capriciousness of their intention could not be very well met or provided for. In his makeshift fort everywhere encircled by darkness, Mr. Lecky did not care to meditate further on the subject.

A remedy for thought was something to read; and Mr. Lecky wished to read now, at once. His desire found him nothing but the booklet of instructions regarding the shotgun. Though this was not what he meant, he produced it, mussed, from his pocket, held its small pages up to the streams of light.

However, there was one other cure for thought. Eventually, quieting, he drowsed, neither reading words, nor fearing to be alone, nor thinking of mad men.

The dark grew thin. Shining uselessly so many hours, the batteries of the lanterns were weakened. Gray light mingled quietly with theirs. Soon they were hardly more than circles of thick, illuminated glass spilling a weak yellow radiance on the table before them.

Mr. Lecky stirred and the muzzle of the shotgun dug him in the armpit. He had laid it by him when he lay down, but much good it would have done him! Shocked to realise that he had fallen soundly asleep without planning to, he could none the less see that everything was in order. Finding himself all right, he must conclude that his danger was not acute. He might, indeed, consider it proved that he had nothing living to fear, since his fort had been all night like a beacon to prowlers and none had come. Rested and cheered, he went yawning into his lavatory.

When he came out Mr. Lecky saw the ham and biscuits, available for his breakfast, with distaste. Today he would devote to collecting food more varied. And perhaps a book, he decided, remembering his last night's desire to read. And—looking at the dying lanterns which he now hastily snapped off—he would do well to depend on candles, if he could find them, for ordinary illumination. He had already largely exhausted eight big batteries.

Hoisting the empty pack basket to his back, Mr. Lecky pushed aside the desk in the corner. He passed through the swinging doors and unhurriedly downstairs. Walking with no caution he put out a hand to swing open the doors on the sixth floor. Here again he was confronted by those square panes of glass placed to prevent the accidental collision of people coming in contrary directions. Chance, or it might be the inherited ghost of a primitive faculty of apprehension, made Mr. Lecky raise his eyes, glance through.


Mr. Lecky's shock was something like that suffered by a man walking, absorbed in other matters, on a level pavement, when he reaches, without having observed it, a step down. The staggering jolt confused Mr. Lecky. He could not, for a second, collect himself enough to draw back. As it happened, his slowness was not important, for the person he saw faced the other way. Standing by the pyramided shelves this man was clumsily intent on twisting back on its key the cover of a sardine tin. When done, he instantly dug out the contents with his fingers, thrust them, animal-like, into his concealed mouth.

Mr. Lecky did step back then, with a stunned, numb delicacy. Although he was not conscious of coming to any

decision, he found himself climbing the stairs, intense thuds
of his heart keeping time to a progress clearly frantic. He
had reached the seventh floor—two steps at a time, from
toe to toe; he was half way to the eighth floor, before the
superhuman energy of his fright was exhausted. He had to
pause a moment and hold the rail. A sense of the careless
folly which had let him overlook his gun joined with the
spasms of so bad a shock and made him ready to weep
with rage. His face was mottled. His breath burnt him.

When he could, he went on. Though his hands were
so weakly inaccurate as to make it actually a convenience,
he was infuriated afresh and shaken into a muffled whisper
of cursing to see more carelessness—the entrance of his
fort left open for anyone to enter. On the steel and polished
stock of his shotgun his swollen fingers were infused with
the quick vibration of his pulse beat. After a moment he
was able to take up the cartridge belt sagging with shells.
He drew it around his waist, let the end slip and swing,
having no free hand. Brought to reason, he laid down the
gun a moment while he buckled the belt in place. Under
it he slid the long blade of the kitchen knife, recovered
his gun. Ready now, it was time to consider his position
and procedure.

To help him in judgment, or perhaps only to alarm
him, Mr. Lecky had his first picture of the unknown adversary. There was a wide thick back, shoulders slightly
hunched, head put down, and hand raised suddenly in the
wolfing of the fish. Posed so, he had been more like a dangerously large ape in man's clothing than a man. Mr.
Lecky began nervously to wet his lips. It might be best
to seize the first opportunity to shoot without warning. It
might not be safe to temporise. A man of the sort he had
seen would be, he was convinced, more than a match for

him in a hand to hand encounter. He must remember, too, that his opponent might prove to be armed, able to return fire or even to fire first.

Mr. Lecky waited, unable to make up his mind. To shoot down a fellow-being, deliberately, from concealment, was an act which his habit of thought held to be atrocious. He could not look forward to the sight of blood—or, possibly more to be dreaded, the sound of suffering—with composure. When he moved, it was hesitantly. A moral squeamishness aggravated the distress of shock and fear. He felt a confusion of foreboding, lest on the one hand, for all his precaution, he be going to his own death; on the other, lest he be setting out to contrive another man's.

Moving this time toward the doors on the far side, Mr. Lecky was embarking on the preliminaries of the plan he did not wish to adopt. It would begin with an approach under cover to a point from which he could observe his adversary. The thought, the idea of observation, was what offered him a loophole of compromise, a covenant to withhold final decision. Accepting it, he saw in addition, or thought he saw, another possibility. Such are the fantasies of never-chastened human wishing that some corner of Mr. Lecky's mind could harbor a hope too sweet to be plausible, too silly to bear conscious consideration, that the prowler among the groceries might have been an hallucination. In the silence of his going downstairs he framed this small, bootless appeal. Coming to the door, he laid his face against the surface of it, brought an eye to the corner of the small window. The creature was beyond dispute still there, still at his feeding.

Mr. Lecky examined him carefully. His enemy's characteristic posture appeared to be a crouch, making his movements at once careless and furtive. Every moment or two he halted, some gesture half complete, to turn his head

and peer about him. Mr. Lecky could then observe the
pallor of a wide face smudged with a few days' growth of
beard. Either the face had no expression, or Mr. Lecky was
not close enough to see any. Except for the mouth, half
open, and eyes moving in their sockets, this strange man
might have been carrying on his shoulders no more than a
somewhat hairy lump of bloodless and fatty meat.

If there was nothing agreeable about this appearance,
there was at the same time a stupid impotence which re-
proached Mr. Lecky with his desperately malicious scheme.
Upstairs, attempting to hit on a plan, Mr. Lecky had been
dealing with a fiction. His new impression worked at once
to fill him with a sense of contemptuous security. The gun,
which he pushed under his arm, became less an instrument
of mastery than a symbol of it. His obvious course was to
step out boldly, challenge and question.

Pushing the door open with no more hesitation, Mr.
Lecky advanced directly through the long series of tables
set with china and glassware. Now that the plan was discarded, he was interested to see that he would have had
no difficulty in getting within easy shooting distance un-
observed. His frank progress did not attract attention until,
conveniently near, he said: *Stand where you are!*


The sound of human speech was startling to Mr. Lecky
himself; but the effect on the person he spoke to was apparently stunning. Whatever knowledge this man might
have had of Mr. Lecky's presence in the store, and whatever good reason it ought to have given him sooner or later
to expect this encounter, he could not have expected it
now. He stood for a moment arrested in the act of reaching
for something on a table. Perhaps he felt that some efficacy
lay in not looking, since thirty seconds must have elapsed

before he let his hand fall. Then, appalling in his slowness, he faced about.

The mouth was still open, the eyes still shifting in the bloodless oval of the big face. He made no attempt either to speak or flee, only raising one hand against his breast and pressing it there as though his shocked heart hurt him. Then, without special sign of conscious volition, he took a mechanical step forward, followed by another. Mr. Lecky said more sharply: *Stand still! I won't hurt you.*

That his mere appearance should so stupefy and awe ought surely to be encouraging; but, instead, the perfection of Mr. Lecky's confidence suffered a trifling impairment. He felt the uncanny prolonging of the man's understandable shock. Mr. Lecky had been waiting for relaxation, the tokens of some natural recovery in eyes and expression to indicate that what he had to say would be heard and apprehended. Viewed in the thin daylight, light enough because Mr. Lecky was now used to it, but not good, the man's face stayed simply blank. Although he did stand still when told to, that seemed to Mr. Lecky more a result of the sharpness of tone given the last words than of any grasp of their meaning. The impression was quickly confirmed. Having paused, as if to let the sound pass, the man began to move. No more than a dozen yards separated them. Alarm, immediate and instinctive, brought the gun into Mr. Lecky's hands, muzzle toward this disobedient person. Mr. Lecky said: *Stand still, or I'll shoot!*

He produced again that unreal, disturbing pause. The best explanation of it actually seemed to be that his opponent was stopping to listen. Mr. Lecky's voice reached and troubled him; he thought he heard something, which he in no way connected with the figure of Mr. Lecky. Plainly he saw Mr. Lecky and meant to find out what he was. Regardless of the gun, he was coming right up to

Mr. Lecky. Just as Mr. Lecky now knew that he would, the man began to move once more in the restored silence. To stop him a noise would be required. Mr. Lecky shouted, not bothering with words. The man stopped.

It could go on indefinitely, or at least—for every pause must be a few feet nearer—until Mr. Lecky was reached. Not wanting that to happen, Mr. Lecky thoughtlessly stepped back, widening the space between them. Now that Mr. Lecky moved, his opponent moved too. Mr. Lecky, dismayed, must realise that this was turning into a pursuit. He cried: *Listen. I don't want to hurt you. But if you come any closer . . .*

His pursuer, Mr. Lecky saw, upset—for he had just assented to the theory that a voice would bring a halt—must now have decided to ignore noises which did him no harm. Mr. Lecky took two steps back and aside, around a counter. What he was looking for, he felt rather than realised, he had finally found. The gun, a moment before so embarrassingly useless as he retreated in the open aisle, resumed its value. He leaned forward, elbows on the counter corner, brought the butt against his shoulder and slid his finger around the trigger. He shouted: *One step more!*

In his agitation he did not wait for that step. Mr. Lecky's finger contracted, encountering a second's surprising, stout resistance. He tugged harder, frightened, and instantly came an explosion.

Its violence was much greater than Mr. Lecky had expected. He closed his eyes, jerking his head away. His improperly held stock dealt his shoulder a blow like a club's. Much to the right, higher, and many diagonal yards behind his pursuer's head, an array of stemmed glassware crowning a row of shelves had gone magically to pieces in the great crash of a gun fired indoors.

Mr. Lecky was too stupefied, both by the loudness of

the report and the totally unforeseen blow to his shoulder, to act further. The man he was shooting at had recoiled as though similarly dazed. Both of them stood in consternation. The intense, convulsive movement of Mr. Lecky's hands performed wholly by accident on action bar latch and sliding chamber the simple gesture of reloading. The empty red shell snapping out the side made him jump, but he guessed with high-strung clarity what it meant. He jerked the slide forward again, crammed the gun against his shoulder and, wincing as he touched the bruise it had just inflicted, said: *Have you had enough?*

Receiving no response, Mr. Lecky took a threatening step into the aisle, and immediately the man wheeled about, starting to run. Mr. Lecky clutched the gun, the barrel shaking badly. This explosion was just as shocking and infinitely more painful to his shoulder, but he did not pause. Running himself, he came into the grocery department, got his dodging quarry in view again, lifted his weapon and pulled the trigger. He had, however, neglected to eject the empty shell. Aghast, he brought himself up a moment before he understood the failure. It took an additional moment to right the matter. When he was ready, the stair doors had already swung. His target had disappeared.

First impulse was to continue the pursuit without delay, for Mr. Lecky was frightened by the unwelcome thought that nothing prevented the fugitive from running up to Mr. Lecky's fort and there arming himself for shooting of his own. Mr. Lecky gained the stair landing with a rush. The man, as he might have guessed one fleeing would, had run down instead of up. The noise of steps and stumbling was unmistakably down, perhaps no more than a flight below. Mr. Lecky threw himself against the rail, tilted his gun, and though he did not know exactly where his quarry was, fired a third shell with a thunder of echoes down the shaft.

This time his shoulder pained him so that he could no longer ignore it. Holding his gun by the warm breech, he tried to ease himself by flexing the muscles, swinging his arm. Treated this way, the pain was actually not great. It was the thought of having to fire again that made him wince. Standing quietly, he could hear the noise below an instant longer, and then silence. That meant, no doubt, entrance into some lower floor, and Mr. Lecky drew breath, the emergency for the instant ended.

Now he had time to notice, a little faint, the forgotten fact that he had not eaten anything. Turning slowly, Mr. Lecky reëntered the grocery department. He could probably eat with entire security now; but, thinking of that, he thought suddenly that sleeping securely would henceforth be impossible. Laying his gun on a small stool, he helped himself to a jar of preserved figs. Abstracted, but working more carefully, or favored by a flaw in the glass, he knocked a quarter inch of the short neck and the vacuum cap neatly off together. Thoughtful, watchful, too, he began to eat, wiping his mouth and chewing slowly. Tired into a sort of calm by his vigorous activity, it was only at this moment that he saw, with the exact certainty of a premonition strongly felt, and from the first moment of the encounter, waiting on his leisure to be recognised, that whatever else his opponent was or was not, he could hardly be altogether sane.

## 5  THE IDIOT HUNT

When he had finished breakfast, Mr. Lecky sat down and rediscovered how to load his shotgun with fresh shells from the cartridge belt. The magazine refilled, Mr. Lecky still hesitated. This time it was not indecision. His decision was made, the issue determined. Other courses might have seemed possible before, but no longer. Between himself and a sane man, not antagonised by hostilities, some understanding or agreement might be reached. With an idiot, frightened and angry, there was only one thing to do. If Mr. Lecky did not find the idiot and settle with him before it became dark, or, at least, before, exhausted, he fell asleep, the idiot would probably find and settle with the drowsing Mr. Lecky.

Seeing this, Mr. Lecky saw too that he had made a serious mistake in allowing the fellow to get off. He ought to have followed, never minding breakfast, his sore shoulder, or anything else, while he still had the sound of flight to guide him. With nothing to guide him, Mr. Lecky stirred uncertainly, went out to the stairs slowly. With concentrated care and attention he began to descend them.

The ground to be covered was so vast that he must eliminate some of it, if possible, and Mr. Lecky decided that it would be safe to ignore the fifth floor. He was certain that he had heard his lunatic go farther than that. Probably farther than the fourth floor, too; but here he was less sure. It would not be wise to let himself be cut

off from his base. As far as the too numerous stairways
would permit, he ought to try to keep the man he hunted
always below him.

Considered with such elaborate caution, the circumstances gave Mr. Lecky no reason to be sure that, while he
ate, his quarry had not retraced his course by stairs out of
sight and hearing. He could have gone above. He could
have found and profitably ransacked Mr. Lecky's ninth-
floor stronghold. Mr. Lecky did not believe that he had;
and, in any event, the chance, like innumerable others,
would have to be taken or he would never get forward
at all.

As soon as he had entered the fourth floor, Mr. Lecky
found himself in departments devoted to children's apparel,
baby carriages, nursery furniture. He walked out on an
open rectangle, floored with dull black linoleum. On four
sides were glass show cases covering set-back shelves
stacked with piles of baby clothes, and for some time he
looked at them, brooding. At length he thought of a sort
of plan.

The plan was for a calculated quartering of the floor,
begun on a fairly direct diagonal line which would bring
him to the far corner. When he reached it, he turned down
along the end and walked across. From this corner he
moved back, intersecting the first diagonal with a second.
The plan's weakness was that his quarry had perfect liberty
to move around a corner or given square of counters and
so stay constantly hidden. However, by this method, Mr.
Lecky would see, before he was through, practically every
square foot of floor space from one angle or another.
Since he half believed that the man he hunted was not
here anyway, and since by no means could he manage to
see every square foot of the floor simultaneously, what he
did was as well-considered as anything he might have done.

None the less, the sort of success which Mr. Lecky suddenly met with must be ascribed to accident. Constantly looking about him, he came again, as his course required, into the central rectangle from which he started. As he began to cross the dark linoleum he happened to look down. His eye, arrested, discovered there, outlined very dimly in dust on the smooth surface, the faint print of a shoeless human foot.

Mr. Lecky stopped short, looked up, then all around him quickly, then down at his shoes. He was convinced, too, that no such mark had been there when last he left the place. A few minutes ago his quarry must have gone through, moving naturally in the direction the foot pointed. Given thus a pointer to the idiot's whereabouts, Mr. Lecky was at the same time given urgent proof of the idiot's to-be-expected and much to-be-feared cunning. The man had taken off his shoes to move more quietly. Inspired, Mr. Lecky stooped and with difficulty put off his own. Drawing the laces of one under his cartridge belt, he knotted them to the laces of the other, pushed the suspended shoes around on his hip, out of the way.

Determining the line of the indicated direction, Mr. Lecky moved at once, tiptoeing with alacrity. He passed between the counters at the corner, very carefully approached the outer edge, and, crouching, peered down the adjoining aisle. The simplicity of it, the complete success of the maneuver, seemed too good to be true. He saw that while his plan of search had apparently been grasped and his movements in carrying it out slyly foreseen, the print on the floor and Mr. Lecky's wise use of it had not been expected nor provided for. At roughly thirty yards, back to Mr. Lecky, the big form of the man he sought was

squatting. He was waiting patiently to see, from his own
angle, Mr. Lecky cross the open space.

With his quarry in full sight, and so utterly unsuspect-
ing, Mr. Lecky managed to be rid of qualms. Not that
he was calm; but his unsteadiness came from an excess of
jubilation. He put his elbows stealthily on the counter,
holding his breath while he aligned the gun as firmly and
exactly as he could to bear on the middle of this quite
large target. Taking the greatest pains not to move the
muzzle or shake the barrel, he crooked his index finger,
drawing hard on the trigger.

This report, unheralded, purposeful and vehement,
whacked out like the crack of doom. The recoil pad, better
and more closely held this time, did take the sharpness off
the stock's recoil, but Mr. Lecky's shoulder was tender
enough to make him grunt. As for the man shot at, who
could doubt that he was hit? The squatting figure, motionless an instant, gave a frightful scream. Immediately
bounding, as though the impact impelled him forward, he
ran, and howled again. The unhampered frenzy with which
his quarry moved dismayed Mr. Lecky, but not so much
as those two shocking cries. Perhaps they were fright only,
for the movement seemed to show that Mr. Lecky had
missed once more; and this was likely. He understood now,
disgruntled, the extreme poorness of his shooting. That he
could have hit fairly and yet failed to cripple did not
occur to him.

Still quailing with absurd compunction, Mr. Lecky let
himself lose important moments. When, recovering from
the idiot's outcries, he did get into motion, running, he was
brought presently to a second senseless halt. A dozen feet
from where his hunted man had crouched, along the line of
flight, Mr. Lecky saw something on the floor. It amounted
to no more than a few wet circular spots, minutely frilled

from the light impact of their fall, but it made him waver, harrowed by even this petty foretaste of his projected bloodshed. While he hesitated, he heard the dull swing of the stair doors and realised that his quarry was on the point of making a second escape. Certainly Mr. Lecky would deserve no more favors from fortune if he threw all the fruits of this one away. Hastily he followed after.

On the third floor were women's clothes. Since all sound had ceased when he gained the stair landing above, Mr. Lecky could be reasonably sure that his idiot must have gone in here. Ready to rush in, too, he stopped himself. A desperate man with no advantage but stature and physical strength might, even though demented, reason that his hope lay in coming to grips. By waiting just inside the swinging doors, he might be able to spring on his opponent, entering, with a suddenness compensating him for all handicaps.

Standing outside, well clear, Mr. Lecky could recognise the great danger he faced. He did not know and could not possibly tell which side his enemy might take. Readiness to fire and no matter how much alertness would avail him little if he guessed the wrong side, pushed the wrong half of the door, looked, for the first fatal moment, the wrong way. His idiot would be within inches of his defenceless back.

As a way out of this quandary Mr. Lecky chose finally a furtive further descent of the stairs, passage through the second floor and up other stairs, in other doors, which his enemy could have no certainty about. The time wasted, in the event that the idiot had prepared no ambush, was clearly a present from Mr. Lecky, giving that much longer to perfect a concealment. However, the whole undertaking,

depending for success on the triumph of Mr. Lecky's intelligence and caution over his opponent's strength and
fury, must be safeguarded from just such hazards as the
closed third-floor doors might offer.

Moving with no noise, Mr. Lecky went on down. Most
of the second floor was occupied by displays of blankets,
bedspreads, sheets and pillow cases; but women's shoes
were here also. That department, with its squares and aisles
of empty chairs gave free passage. There were no places
of possible cover which Mr. Lecky need be cautious in passing. Out, and up the opposite stairway, he regained the
third floor. He made a quick inspection through the glass,
gave the doors an experimental push, holding his gun
ready while he drew back to see what happened. Nothing
happened; so he went in.

The search confronting Mr. Lecky here promised to be
still more difficult than the one he had undertaken on the
fourth floor. Display and sale of women's wear was more
specialised, more elaborately treated and subdivided. Departments or sections imitated, in some instances, small
shops, having, although roofless, walls, arched doorways,
even show windows, of their own. There were, too, in almost all parts, great numbers of small fitting-rooms not
unlike the eighth-floor ones which Mr. Lecky had used to
make his first, never-occupied fort. Though it might be
shortsighted of a fugitive to hide in places of that sort—
found, no escape would remain—Mr. Lecky viewed them
only in terms of their disadvantage to him, the hunter.
He did not want to trap his idiot that way, at close quarters.
He wanted to see him at a short but safe distance and
shoot him down.

To this difficulty of so many places to hide was added
another almost as great by the bad light and heavy shadows which the complicated partitioning threw in all direc-

tions. Mr. Lecky's hunt here would have every likelihood of proving futile. It could not possibly be planned. He would have to cast about at random in the constant danger of being himself surprised.

However, he might perhaps eliminate the part of the floor where he stood at the moment. An extensive array of fitting-rooms ought to be examined, but otherwise the furnishings were mainly counters for the sale of lingerie. Going by what he imagined he himself would do, Mr. Lecky decided that the idiot would never lurk here when so many places in which it would be harder to find him were close by. Trying to carry this process of putting himself in the idiot's place further, Mr. Lecky was at loss. Rushing in himself, he would have been as likely to go right as left. He took a few half-hearted steps, as though running and about to hide, but it was clearly not possible consciously to do the unconscious. He thought then of crossing to the other door and looking for more blood spots.

Going over there, he looked carefully, but he could not see anything. The man he hunted must have found some way to check his tell-tale bleeding. Mr. Lecky, gazing about him, examining without much hope, and so perfunctorily, possible corners and passages, took a long time to move through the display cases. Often the light was so bad that he might not have seen blood even if it were there. The floor was wood, largely covered by dull-colored thick carpeting, and dusty socks would leave no more prints. Mr. Lecky pushed his gun under his arm, stood still. After his interlude of more direct action he could hardly compel himself to take up the weary business of an extended, disorganized search.

Reluctance to proceed, mother of more inventions than necessity, now helped him a little. He did not know where the idiot was; but, at the same time, perhaps the hidden idiot did not know where Mr. Lecky was. He stepped to the edge of an aisle. It ran almost the length of the department, and at the end, perhaps a hundred yards away, he could see in the gloom the long liquid surface of a full-length mirror. Raising his gun, he fired at this, point blank.

The mirror did not come down in the cascade of metallic-backed glass which he had expected. Mr. Lecky thought at first that he must have missed; but, advancing quickly, he was soon close enough to see that the once flawless surface was clouded and starred from many points. The phenomenon so astonished him that he stood a moment bewildered. For the first time he really understood that he was not, as he foolishly thought, shooting a bullet the size of his gun's muzzle, but a cloud of pellets from a load so light that it was insignificant at that range. In this amazement he could hear, forgetful of its importance, the violent sound of the movement, which he had fired in the very hope of provoking, from his concealed quarry.

In another moment he would lose, through surprise over a stupid irrelevancy, all that his stratagem had gained him. Mr. Lecky broke into a heavy pounding rush which served him for running. He snapped over the action lever, ejecting the shell as he went, and holding the gun in both hands, tilted it carelessly toward the ceiling, firing again, snapping out another shell. He rounded a make-believe house corner representing a shop and had, to his delight, his fleeing idiot distantly in view. Without stopping or making any formal effort to take aim, he brought his gun up and fired once more.

This time Mr. Lecky shot, unafflicted by nervous preparations, with no time for complicated miscalculations, and, as occasionally happens, where he shot was exactly where he looked. The shriek of his target promptly established the rightness of this technique, and, exultant, Mr. Lecky tried it again. Now, unfortunately, he merely repeated his error upstairs in the grocery department. Ejecting the empty shell was not second nature to him; excitement precluded remembering so much. The trigger pin clicked uselessly on the already punched firing cap.

In a frenzy of chagrin Mr. Lecky fumbled for the slide. His quarry plunged into a side aisle, taking himself out of sight; but, belatedly pursuing, Mr. Lecky saw that some fresh source of blood had been tapped—much more copious. This time he stopped with deliberate consideration. His shooting was getting results, but slowly. With a trail so plain to follow, he could afford to wait a moment, fill up his magazine. To rely on the one shot left to meet who knew what emergency would be ridiculous. He laid the gun on the nearest counter and began to press shells out of the webbed loops of his belt.

The shells fitted with exasperating snugness. Mr. Lecky had to grasp the belt in one hand and from the bottom work each shell up with his thumb. The awkwardness of the operation, added to his attempted haste, and hampered, when it was, by shells already removed and still held, made him drop two while he struggled with a fourth. Both of the dropped shells rolled, perversely, in different directions. But not so different that, stepping to snatch up one, Mr. Lecky's agitated foot could not kick the other three yards farther. With the fourth now out, he dropped that, too. Infuriated by such an ill-timed minor delay, he scrambled after them, bent, gasping, and picked up one and then the other. Turning, his unprepared eyes stunned him with a sight of the most horrible sort.

Insane or not, wounded or not, the man he hunted must have realised in the wild carelessness of desperation that his murder would be the end of this chase, that it might pay as well boldly to risk death at once as to suffer death helplessly later. He had, in incredible fact, simply doubled about the long counter. Coming without sound on his unshod feet, supporting himself against the counter with a red-streaked hand, his pale forehead and wide jowl swung forward, he meant to have Mr. Lecky's neglected gun.

Had he been quicker, less cautious perhaps, injured less, or had the fallen shells rolled as little as a foot farther, he might have succeeded. Mr. Lecky could have fainted on the breast-splitting diastole, his heart's frantic dilation. Mr. Lecky jumped. His fingers caught the stock of the shotgun, dragged it clattering over wood and glass into safety. His adversary, forestalled, had made a snatch for it, too; but it was automatic, ineffective by a yard, and he saved himself from falling only with the grip of his bloody hand. Mr. Lecky, delirious in relief and fear, retreated fast, putting space between himself and this clutching, staggering enemy. He came suddenly to his senses. He jabbed his finger through the trigger guard. He jerked the butt against his sore shoulder. He swung up the muzzle, and, the distance being no greater than ten yards, fired directly at the face of the idiot, immobile in stupor or despair, eyes doggedly fixed on him.

Although at this distance it was hardly necessary to aim, Mr. Lecky came as close as possible to missing. The load had no time to scatter in pattern, but its circumference at thirty feet was slightly greater than at the muzzle and by this fine margin Mr. Lecky hit, ploughing a hundred minute balls lightly off the side of his enemy's face and making a wound everything but fatal.

Mr. Lecky's quarry had gone down, forward on his hands and knees, but he was able with insane adroitness to crawl to his feet and flee away. He shrieked again; a sort of

liquid death poured in Mr. Lecky's ear. Hoarse and form-
less, its high pitch broke into an airless loud whimper
which went audibly with him, involuntary and purposeless.

Mr. Lecky stood still, swallowing. His mouth was awash
with spittle which seemed permeated by a flavor like
sucked copper and the taste of the gunpowder which he
could smell. His failure to pursue was not due to prudence
reminding him that his gun was entirely empty. Reason,
overpowered, poleaxed, by the faculty of sight, left him in
a queasy daze, unwillingly reviewing what he had seen
of that lucky shot's work. Larger, unutterably clearer and
more detailed, he beheld again, pushing a damp hand uncertainly against his own face, the magic pulping of that
wide cheek and jaw—skin and flesh in sudden shreds and
tatters, no time yet even to be bloody. Down from the
comminuted orbit hung the bedraggled eyeball. Half a
face was entirely destroyed.

Mr. Lecky watched this image crowding on him in
monstrous anamorphosis. The butt end of his gun hit the
floor, but he held it swinging, and held the counter edge
with his other hand. Convulsed and choking, he vomited
between them on the floor.

. . . *However, the toilet of the wound should be made for
the purpose of relieving it of all kinds of débris (broken
teeth, fragments deprived of periosteum, shreds of soft
tissue) and above all to forestall secondary hemorrhage.
The latter, in fact, results most often from the presence of
traumatizing splinters, and it is generally the lingual artery
that is torn by them in the floor of the mouth. To practise
this toilet no sort of anesthesia, no bistoury, no curette, is
needed. The fingers and a pair of forceps nearly always
suffice. The free splinters are lifted out, in places a still
adherent shred of periosteum is detached, to be left in the*

*wound; sometimes a cut with scissors is necessary to free a*
*poorly detached shred; sometimes again the pointed end of*
*a utilizable fragment is taken off with a rongeur. . . .*

Mr. Lecky, a clown in his unwonted rôle of hunter (he
wiped his mouth now; spat out the sour slime left by his
vomiting) was no better fitted for that of physician; yet,
having done his poor best to kill, having at least succeeded
in guaranteeing his own safety by maiming and half blind-
ing his enemy, Mr. Lecky now felt that he must make
haste after the idiot, bearing this time ignorant and unskilled succor.

By lacking the composure to ask what he purposed
doing once he had come up with his quarry, Mr. Lecky
helped himself into movement. Using the phrase common
for emergencies which one is unequipped, or at first sight,
unable, to meet, Mr. Lecky told himself that he must do
something. Since all he could do was follow after, without thinking or troubling to bring his gun, he did that.

Probably he had heard, not noticing, the stair doors
swing, for he went to them without question, not even
bothering to see the blood on the floor. On the landing,
in better light, the liberal confirming traces of his opponent's passage were harder to overlook. Leaning on the
rail, Mr. Lecky heard the unspeakable drag and thump of
a progress down. He could hear too—though hardly able
to let himself listen, his tongue contorted in his mouth as
though he might block his ears from the inside—the gasping, imperfectly shaped whimper.

Mr. Lecky went down. On the landing of the second
floor he got the injured man in sight and stopped again.
One hand was laid distractedly to the torn face; the other,
on the rail, sliding, locking with tenacity, held the idiot

while he swayed, coming half around, his head against the banisters. Then, somehow recovering, he slipped and staggered a few steps more. Under Mr. Lecky's cheeks the muscles set themselves in a kind of cramp, narrowing his eyes, flaring out his nostrils, lodging his teeth in his lower lip. A nauseated revulsion made it seem impossible for him to move his feet in the direction of this bleeding monster. He opened his mouth and cried: *Wait! I won't hurt you.*

The irony of such a promise from him was not lost on Mr. Lecky. Even the idiot ought not to be fool enough to accept it after suffering so terrible a sample of Mr. Lecky's good will toward him. Mr. Lecky was shaken suddenly. He felt a tremulous convulsion of the diaphragm which he did not recognise, for a moment of high hysteria, as the giggling it actually was. He shouted again: *Wait! I want to help you.*

Nothing was accomplished but an acceleration of the injured man's pace. In point of increased speed, it was negligible; but the frenzy of effort which went into it was appalling. Abruptly Mr. Lecky was able to move again, and he descended, almost running. The injured man reached the bottom barely a yard ahead of him, staggered, his hand on the post, and collapsed, half against it, half on the open flooring of the stair shaft.


Mr. Lecky sat down on the second step, his forearms resting on his knees, his hands hanging. After a while he noticed his stockingless feet, and detached the shoes from his belt, putting them slowly on. By looking a little to the left, through the thin steel balusters of the stair rail, he could see his victim huddled on the floor. The face was fortunately turned from him. Visible were only the obese mounds of sagging shoulders and inert, ungainly buttocks.

Mr. Lecky needed to rest; but he sat there after he no longer needed to, for here was the end of his chase and there was nothing he could do—he did not know how to do anything.

The idiot's labored hoarse breathing made, minute after minute, a sound Mr. Lecky did not like. It might be due, he thought, agitated by it, to the position. That seemed to Mr. Lecky cramped and unnatural. Mr. Lecky got to his feet. Gingerly, with quaking, fastidious recoil, he finally made himself put his hands on the idiot to try to ease him or straighten him out. Except in so far as the gross bulk hampered him, this was not hard, for the body lay lax and inert. However, straining and tugging, Mr. Lecky restored his patient to a sort of consciousness. The idiot began faintly and slobberingly to shriek.

Mr. Lecky shrank back. He stood a moment wringing his useless hands, racking his empty brains. He thought distractedly of making a bandage of something, but he could not help seeing that the idiot's injuries were beyond such simple repair. In his anguish of inability, he could have howled himself, joining the injured man's outcries.

Mr. Lecky could not stand any more noise. That was the resolution of his difficulty, and the whole matter simplified itself. Mr. Lecky looked about him, rubbing his hands on his clothes, and one hand encountered accidentally what he was looking for. He went on his knees. Forcibly he turned the shattered face away, set his hand on the other cheek and bore down. The kitchen knife he took from his belt, and, though he ground his teeth with desperate distaste, he began, not hesitating, to cut, driving the point into the thick neck and pulling it stolidly from left to right.

The edge was sharp enough, and, though Mr. Lecky was not very neat nor very quick, the operation was at length completed. There would be no more noise. Blood, surprisingly copious, widened out steadily on the floor, disgusting Mr. Lecky more than it horrified or dismayed him. He wiped the blade on the man's coat and laid it on the end of a step. Getting painfully to his feet, he looked about once more.

To bury his dead would be difficult. He could not dig. Yet his mind worked for him now with unemotional clarity. He stooped and took up one limp leg, drew the foot under his arm. Dragging hard, he bent forward, pulling the body to the doors. He went slowly, bowed with labor, down the wide cross aisle to the head of the basement stairs in the silverware department. There he breathed a moment, glancing around him, observing attentively, but without trepidation, the information booth, the hanging department signs, the high ventilating grills, the big bell on the pillar. Perfect quiet of desertion lay over everything.

Using his foot, Mr. Lecky pushed his load off the top step. It rolled heavily, rested half way to the landing. This did not satisfy Mr. Lecky, for it could be seen from the top. He went down and pushed it farther. Grunting and shoving, he got it across the landing and sent it tumbling to the bottom, where it brought up, supported against the stair rail.

Mr. Lecky reasoned that his gunfire often repeated, announcing his arrival in floor after floor, would have brought out other lurking foes, had any been there. Thus he rid himself of the distrust which might make him attempt some impossible vigil after this exhausting day. Of other concerns he had none. Finally reaching his fort, he was in no way conscience-stricken to know himself a murderer, and to see in the last light, dry on his hands, the dirty stain of blood. Washing in the lavatory, his hands did not incarnadine more than a minute's flow of water. Here, where no one could take him, force out his guilt, and kill him for it, Mr. Lecky felt no more remorse than Cain, his prototype. He dried his hands on the end of a roll of coarse paper meant for towels. He went out and fumbled in the dark shadows until he found his torches. Though they were much less convenient than the largely used-up lanterns, they would stand on their ends if he did not shake the table.

These strong shafts of light struck the white ceiling and were reflected back. Mr. Lecky could see well enough to eat. He brought his chair over and sat down gratefully while he consumed, but with appetite now, the ham and biscuits which he had disdained in the morning. Even the fact that he was using to cut his ham the knife which had cut a human throat did not disturb him. He had taken care to see that the blade was wiped clean. Sunk in the content of rest after labor, he thought again of the candles he had meant to get, of the book to read, but his failure to have them was no inconvenience. He would not need light long; nor did he wish to read tonight.

Stretching on his cot, the darkness soothed Mr. Lecky. He put a flashlight where he could reach it, but when his mind, fussing in normal protest against so much bodily ease, recalled to him that he had left his gun down on the third floor, he shrugged a little, not enough disturbed, and giving it no further heed, very soon slept.

It was day when Mr. Lecky awoke. He opened his eyes without starting; he did not experience the usual falling qualm of apprehension. He stirred, finding himself stiff from yesterday's exertions. His right shoulder was, in fact, extremely sore. Sitting up, he rubbed it tenderly; yet the pain it caused him was unessential, mere surface twinges. Fundamentally he felt well and alert, confident in his new security. He was pleasantly aware that today he would be free to make a thorough examination of the riches of the extraordinary domain now his. Never in his life having been able to own or enjoy quite enough of anything which cost more than the most trifling sum of money, the thought that now he had everything excited him. He got promptly to his feet and went into his lavatory.

Returning, he swung on his pack basket, walked out, cheerfully, and downstairs to the grocery department and as good a breakfast as he could find. Eating it, he gave up his first idea, which had been to fill the basket with food. That was a waste of energy. Since no one could prevent or interrupt him, it would be easy to come down here for meals. Eating, he could reflect, too, on the great benefit which any means of cooking would be to his diet.

Somewhere, surely, he might find tinned fuel, for use in circumstances like his.

Candles (he still had in mind yesterday's list of things he needed) were to be found on the seventh floor. Mr. Lecky walked leisurely up there after breakfast. Discovering them in great quantities, drawers full of many colored ones in many shapes and sizes, he filled his basket with the largest—tapers perhaps two inches in diameter, wrapped in tissue paper. Each should burn brightly for a long while. He carried up the load and deposited it on the table in his fort.

This took only a little while, but the tinned fuel he had thought of would undoubtedly be in the basement with hardware and household supplies. Mr. Lecky hesitated a moment, remembering what else was there, but his frown was purely practical. He was not satisfied with his disposal of the dead man. Soon the body, beginning to rot, would stink. A better idea would have been to take it and shut it up in some closet or lavatory; yet, on the whole, it might not matter a great deal. Mr. Lecky would spend most of his time many flights upstairs, and the putrefaction could hardly contaminate more than the immediately surrounding atmosphere. If he got today what he needed down there, Mr. Lecky would not have to know anything about it.

Acting quickly, as though minutes might make a difference in whether or not he were greeted below by some revolting stench, Mr. Lecky pushed a flashlight through his belt, resumed his basket, and reaching for it, remembered about his gun. He could stop on the third floor and get it—but on the way up, he decided, for there was no reason to carry it around with him. On the way up, too, he could stop and take a book to read from the department on the main floor.

The task of looking, with the spot of a flashlight, through the dark immensities of the basement for a few small cans, which Mr. Lecky was, at best, only presuming were there, had natural difficulties. In the stair shaft, walking downstairs in the strong white light of the fused glass, a faint shadow before him, the basket on his back squeaking casually with each step, he had anticipated no particular difficulty; but, arrived on the main floor, he saw with disapproval the wide dark stain on stair-shaft pavement, the dried smears and spots of a track passing through the doors. He turned at once, walked back to stairs as far as possible from those in the silverware department.

Mr. Lecky went down without reluctance; but in the confusing darkness he found it hard to be easy and unhurried, for he saw that this search might take hours. He passed quickly through a corner where his moving light fell over kitchen tables and enamelled cabinets. Nor did he want complicated frames for drying laundry in a small space, little stands to aid in the cleaning of shoes, or ranks of folding step-ladders. Inquiringly shifted, his light showed him next, gardening utensils, coiled lengths of rubber hose, piled sacks of chemical fertilizer. Some of the counters were cut into binfuls of different dry bulbs, bags of grass seed, small paper envelopes containing seeds of the vegetables and flowers pictured in color on them. These were of no use to Mr. Lecky.

Traveling on, the shaft of his light reached now a great, dully shining oblong, and he stopped, surprised. Then, through the glass sides, he saw bright shapes of fish wheel in schools down the opaque water, startled by the illumination. Coming at last, and so suddenly, on life like his own, Mr. Lecky moved closer. The fixed flood of his light enveloped these small fish dimly, glowed back on him. They came sliding, drifting, mouths in motion, gills rip-

pling, up the light, against the glass. Their senseless round
eyes stared at Mr. Lecky. Idling with great grace, the extravagant products of selective breeding—fringetails, Ko-
rean, calico—passed, swayed about, came languidly back.
Moving faster, stub-finned, crop-tailed danios from the
Malabar coast appeared, hovered, taking the light on their
fat flanks, now spotted, now iridescent pearl or opal.

Seeing so many of them, so eager and attentive, Mr.
Lecky felt an unexpected compunction. He was their only
proprietor; and soon, trapped unnaturally here in the big
tank, they would starve to death. His light went back to a
counter he had just passed, showing him again the half-
noticed packages—food for birds and pet animals, food too
for fish. Returning to the tank, his light found many of
the fish still waiting, the rest rushing back. He went and
took a package, tore the top off, and poured the contents
onto the rectangle of open water. It would perhaps post-
pone the time when, having eaten each other, the sick re-
mainder must die anyway.

Mr. Lecky dropped the empty package. In the dark a
curious low sound reached him from beyond the tank. He
jumped about, his light going with him. There was silence,
and then suddenly, bringing them to his attention, from a
long line of hanging bird cages, a chirping, a brush of
feathers and flap of stretched wings. Uncertainly followed
a few thin bursts of song, as though Mr. Lecky's light had
persuaded some of the birds that a new day was dawning.
Accepting this added responsibility, Mr. Lecky went over
and, passing down the line, found and opened one after
another the cage doors. No birds came out, but hunger
might eventually make them come out. Being able to fly
at will, they could perhaps find food among the seeds.

Impatient at the time he had wasted on these merciful
acts, Mr. Lecky moved on into a section full of bathroom

fixtures: racks, soap dishes, cabinets on the wall whose mirrors turned back at him the bright circle of his light and a glimpse of his own pale face behind. Now he was approaching the front, and he halted, for after all, he had been here before. The stairs were over there, and at the foot of them lay the carcass of his idiot. Mr. Lecky shot his light that way in a hasty, unplanned movement. The stairs jumped out of the dark just where he had imagined they would be; but they were too distant for any exact scrutiny. Turning sharply, Mr. Lecky crossed the whole width of the floor.

Paints and varnishes piled up in orderly labelled rows on shelves along the side. Near here, if anywhere, Mr. Lecky was inspired to realise, would be his tinned fuel; and, as he walked, paint finally gave way to polishes, waxes and cleaning fluids. Just beyond them, he beheld, triumphant, what he wanted. Shrugging off his pack basket, shifting the flashlight from hand to hand, he took down the cans. On the counter stood a metal frame with two of the cans in position beneath it, showing how it would serve as a flimsy, improvised stove. He seized that too, folding the legs under and thrusting it in his basket.

Next, he should carefully consider whether he wanted anything else down here; but if he did want anything, his mind, obsessed abruptly with the desire to get up into the light, would not think of it for him. Shouldering his basket, he started off for the stairs.

Mr. Lecky had proceeded quickly for several moments before he drew up, shocked. A few more steps and he might have stumbled on his idiot, for the stairs he had been approaching were the front stairs to the silverware department, which he wished to avoid. Shaken by this unpleasant mistake, he re-directed himself, turning back down

the center of the dark floor. Certainly he did not want to
see the corpse; the corpse could not very well want to see
him.

However narrowly, the ghastly meeting had after all
been avoided. Safe up in the good enough light of the
main floor, Mr. Lecky's relief made him cheerful. He was
now reminded of the book he had planned to get.


It was the habit of his years of security prevailing over
more recent but brief experience which made Mr. Lecky so
poor an observer. On his way back here, intent on his er-
rand downstairs, he had given little attention to his sur-
roundings. Coming up again, he was surprised to step out
on the edge of a department where nothing but books was
sold. Books were all around him, solidly packing the
shelves on the walls, stacked in rows and tiers and mounds
on every table.

Putting off his basket, Mr. Lecky began at random to
handle the books on the first table. So many of them made
him doubtful, for while he wanted a book, he wanted it
only if he could be fairly sure that his trouble in reading it
would be repaid. He examined the clean jackets; he let the
new pages run past his fingers. Turning the leaves of a
book, he could sometimes judge from the proportion of the
broken lines of conversation to solid and unbroken para-
graphs whether the work would be tedious to read. Still at
loss he saw finally a volume whose paper jacket bore the
arresting silhouette of a nude woman. He snapped it open,
to face page after page of closely printed words without
dialogue. However, the jacket picture seemed to promise a
subject matter which he could read with attention. Satisfied, he pushed it into his basket, only mildly embarrassed

to find himself yielding to so improper an urge. After all, there was no one here to shame him by the discovery of his low choice.

His sharp appetite suggested luncheon.


When he had eaten (he would put off attempting to prepare a warm meal for himself until evening), Mr. Lecky, in the lavatory, looked at a mirror. Unless he purposed to grow a beard he must do something about shaving; and faced with this annoyance, he wondered why not have a beard. Every day for years he had frustrated the efforts of his physical organism to provide him with one, never checking nor discouraging the attempt, so it seemed certain that he could grow whiskers on his face. The novelty of the idea interested him. It might give him a more imposing appearance.

Transferring his attention from his face, already darkened by the neglected first stubble of sprouting hair on cheeks and chin, he saw that he ought to get himself new clothes. He ought to throw away these garments, worn, torn, spoiled with dust and spilled food and dried blood. There was no reason why he should not have all the clothes he wanted. More, if he chose, than he could ever use, a splendid super-abundance of garments—selected, furthermore, because he fancied them, not because they promised to wear well, be slow to show how dirty they were, and attract no attention by undue individuality or brightness.

Descending promptly to the fifth floor, Mr. Lecky entered the men's clothing department. Sliding back the wide glass doors of a case, he took out a suit. Removing the coat from the form that held it and laying the trousers on a chair, he took off his own disreputable coat and thrust an

arm into the sleeve of the new one. It was a great deal too
small.

Mr. Lecky noticed, however, that a cardboard oblong
was sewed lightly to the cuff. On it was printed a number,
plainly the price, a number which must mean size, and a
number with no meaning Mr. Lecky could guess. A higher
size number might be a larger garment. Pushing the door
all the way back, Mr. Lecky took up the hanging sleeves,
consulting the successive cards. They ran, he found, in obvious progression, increasing finally in size enough for
even his inexperienced eye to note it. He took down what
he judged would be more nearly right.

This coat was easy to get into. The sleeves neither
stopped half way down his forearms nor extended so far
as to obstruct the use of his hands. Buttoning it, he found
that the cloth drew tightly over his abdomen; but this was
a difficulty he very often had even when someone assisted
his selection. The slight feeling of constraint gave him a
not unpleasant sense of being girded up, made more compact and efficient. Had there been anyone to say it to, Mr.
Lecky might easily have said that this would do, self-
consciously brusque and indifferent—perhaps the more so,
because the cloth, while answering the factitious requirements of the dinginess and probable durability, did not
please him in the least.

Even now it would do. He might as well take it, since
there need be no limit to the number he could have. Drop-
ping it, he turned to seek his size in cabinets where the
garments were higher priced and presumably better. Engaged thus, pulling out the sleeves, holding up the cards
to see them and the cloth, he took down a suit from time to
time, tossed it out on the floor. He was absorbed in the
petty pleasure of gratifying his liberated taste. He had

found his number on the sleeve of a rough tweed coat,
checked brown, as nearly as the light served him, almost to
the point of orange. Bringing it out, he removed his trousers, ready to pull on the trousers supplied here. Still holding the coat, he stopped then, aware by a sudden instinctive
horripilation of his skin and tightening of his scalp that
something surely terrible was in progress.

*. . . the Egyptians after their feastings and carousings
caused a great image of death to be brought in and shewed
to the guests and bystanders, by one that cried aloud . . .*

Mr. Lecky's realisation had been delayed. It was necessary
to tear his attention away from what he was doing and give
it to what seemed only a minor distraction, or at most, a
baseless foreboding. He stirred and roused himself, feeling
the foreboding rather than hearing the sound. An instant
passed, and he began to hear as well as feel. Muffled by
distance, but clamorous wherever it was, and carrying far
through the store below him in the stillness, an electric bell
rang peal on reiterated resonant peal.

The vibration of it seemed to be left hanging on the air
everywhere after it suddenly stopped and the brief persistence of this echo gave the whole ringing unreality. Conscious of himself standing just as the sound had surprised
him, in graceless undergarments showing his fat and hairy
legs, and the shirt hanging its loose tails below his rump,
Mr. Lecky lifted his foot and began to put the trousers on.
He took the coat and put that on.

Almost sure that he could not have heard any such thing,
Mr. Lecky was none the less still listening. He was re-
warded by soon detecting the slight steady ringing in his
own ears. Strained for and studied, it became loud, as loud

as a distant bell, especially when there was no bell to ring
and no one to ring a bell. Mr. Lecky's spirits tried to rise a
little in relief. This explanation was obviously the right
one, yet, restive and curious, his thought drew away from
it, traveled skipping from floor to floor down, down, and
Mr. Lecky recoiled, closing his hands, able to see the high
sprinkler valves, the ventilating grills, the information
booth, the silver in the counters, and, on the pillar by the
basement stairs, the round gong, the perforated square
magnet and coil box. . . .

Mr. Lecky gave over his clothes-collecting. He left everything and walked upstairs.

Regaining the ninth floor, Mr. Lecky found himself on
the far side, distant by the whole furniture-crowded department from his fort. What change had overtaken him,
Mr. Lecky did not know. Never before had he entered here
without a desire to put himself inside his defences. His
coming up must have been with the assumption that so he
wished to do now; but he did not. His circle of furniture
suggested only a pen or a prison. In the gloom of its
added shadows he would have nothing to do but sit and
listen.

He paused. He moved on. His feet were taking him
there. He could not reason with such an urge; he could
only resist it a little by going a long way. From the stair
doors he passed down the side, looking in at a series of
open-sided rooms where pieces picked from the scattered
displays on the floor had been arranged in formal, deserted
tableaux, to show them as they would look, or might best
look, in apartments where people actually lived.

Mr. Lecky's reluctance to get where he was going let
him glimpse, although inattentively, with impotent appreciation, the setting for lives less strait, more expensive and
easier than his own had ever been. To wash and relieve his

natural wants merely as a matter of course in such a bathroom as he passed now—and stopped, in spite of everything, to look at again—might epitomize Mr. Lecky's
mortal hopes. The utilitarian fixtures were all of pale-
yellow porcelain. Mirrors, glass doors, polished stone wain-
scoting, reflected what light they caught.

Perhaps he stood too long, losing his anxiety, for, not
starting, but with the same previous slow realisation, Mr.
Lecky knew that his bell was ringing impatiently. It was a
little fainter; it must, indeed, proceed from the point he had
thought of far below. He turned in a sad stupor, as though
he hoped to see the line of the sound's approach. Soon it
stopped.

## 7  THE TABLE IN THE WILDERNESS

The idiot lay downstairs in the hole Mr. Lecky had chosen
for him. Mr. Lecky, upstairs, went to his fort. Arriving, he
saw in the gloom and touched the things he had that morning brought there. They had lost savor now. They promised nothing. He picked up this, to set it down and take
that, shaking his head from side to side. A mortal ennui,
coming to live with him, made its residence by tossing out
the small baggage of Mr. Lecky's plans and desires. His
brain was void of purpose, airless, chill as an empty house.

Brooding, he sat still, bemused by nothing while time
passed and the afternoon ended slowly. As far as he was

consciously or intellectually concerned, he might have sat
forever in the luxury and insentience of despair. Yet to
brood, to despair, even to sit, he must be fed. There was
no relief from this endless schedule of food; and if he could
or would not think to provide himself, his belly could pro-
mote the reflexes which, without his thinking, would provide for him.

Mr. Lecky was going downstairs. Under his arm he
pressed the light metal frame of his stove. He carried two
cans of fuel, an electric torch, and, angling out his coat
pocket, a thick candle. He had left matches in his discarded
suit. Since his stomach was ready for food, he went to get
matches, so that he could cook. When he had found them,
he returned to the sixth floor and, still inconscient, set
about his supper.


He had no pot to cook in, and no implement to open a can.
The latter Mr. Lecky found. Such things he looked for in
drawers, and so now he opened what drawers he saw until,
unsurprised, he discovered an instrument which would take
off bottle caps, rip tin, draw corks. He lit his taper then.
Holding it at an angle, he let the liquefied paraffin spill on
the table until there was enough to harden and hold the
candle erect. By this light he cleared a space and set up
his stove.

Prying the lids from the fuel cans he put them in place.
The candle flame grew brighter while he did it, and he
stood regarding its shaking, sharp-pointed spatula, dumbly
observing the short work it made of darkness. Turning
finally he glanced at the illuminated shelves encircling the
pillar behind him. That they should be lined with the repe-
titious labels of soup tins stirred a spark of interest, a
surprised appreciation. His experience resigned him un-

reasonably to the idea that what was convenient or to be desired would always be found far away, after irksome effort. The can opener made one, and this made two things as convenient as possible.

Twenty sorts of soup stood there, and several brands. Mr. Lecky's interest did not extend to making a choice, and the mere fact that a choice could be made reduced him, for a moment, to helplessness. Finally, spurred by the appetite to which he was indifferent, he took any one, read the printing on the parti-colored label of paper. He held the soup can like a skull; and at once he did not want it. The soup was made from celery. Mr. Lecky put it back. He stood in mild misery, harassed again by the plague of a will impotent in its restored freedom.

If the mind cannot direct, it can be cunning to protect its ease. Mr. Lecky now proposed a fantastic pact to himself. He shut his eyes. He reached again and took a can. Eyes still shut, he ripped the label from it, crumpled and threw away the paper. Now he could not tell what he had until he opened it.

He touched a struck match to the waxy surface of the substance filling a fuel tin. The heat melted it. The resulting liquid caught in a lifting swirl of insubstantial violet flame. Over this fire, on the frame of the little stove, he placed his can. With no thought of the blind and terrible force so simply and stupidly to be evoked, Mr. Lecky moved about, compelling himself to think of other things to fetch for his meal. At intervals he stood and watched, innocently hoping that his can was getting hotter. Finally he put out a finger to see if it were hot. He did not touch it, for he did not have to. Put near, his finger tips felt the radiations of sheet steel under the titanic stress of steam. The microscopic structure, its cohesion jeopardized, was

shaking like jelly. Mr. Lecky bent down to blow out the
colored flame.

Swirling, it flattened away before his breath, but it had
a tenacity of its own and Mr. Lecky straightened up, defeated. He would slide the cover over the fiery mouth, he
decided, and extinguish it that way. Now, he reached for
the cover, and chance was surely his friend again. Had his
face been down there, to meet the outrageous explosion
half way, he might have got it all. As it was, only a little
of the scalding mess of vegetables, flying fanwise, spat-
tered his neck and the side of his head.

Mr. Lecky gasped in anguish multiple and breath-taking.
He pawed away the vegetable débris, clinging venomous
with its saturating steam, and burned his fingers. He took
a few blind steps. He corrected himself, thinking of cold
water. He stumbled against a table in the shadows and
precipitated an avalanche of the small articles piled there.
He could not find the lavatory door, but the porcelain bowl
of the drinking fountain came to his eye. He clutched at it,
shot up its jet of water, swung his stinging cheek and neck
back and forth across this minute stream.

The cool wetness did afford relief—enough to stay the
immediate thoughtless impulse of anguish, and so to allow
Mr. Lecky to remember that water would only end by aug-
menting the smart. Some salve or ointment, oiling the
scalded skin and shutting out the air was what he needed.
Any such thing would be found far below among drugs
and what were called toilet articles on the main floor.

Five minutes ago Mr. Lecky would not have gone anywhere, could not have brought himself to seek a hundred
yards for anything. He was enlivened now. Void then of
desire, he was now filled up by pain, given the most en-
grossing kind of absorption. Neither darkness nor distance

impressed him. He held his hand against his throbbing neck, returning to the scene of his small disaster with brisk, purposeful haste. He took his flashlight from the table. A sharp smell of burnt vegetables came to him, but the flame in the fuel tin had been smothered. Leaving only the solitary candle burning, he went, the shaft of light hopping along the floor in front of him, to the stair doors.

On this business or that, Mr. Lecky had traversed before most of the front sections of the main floor; so he knew where to go to find what he wanted. Even if he had not known, he might have been guided as he passed directly toward the back by the slow suffusing of the air with one general odor of many mixed scents—soap and perfumes. The beam of his light twitched up, swinging through the middle air. It picked out a hanging oblong of glass on which gold letters spelled PROPRIETARY MEDICINES.

Mr. Lecky soon stepped behind a counter and began to open the deep lower drawers, sending his light over piles of boxed tubes of tooth pastes, shaving creams, cold creams, ointments, until he found one of the last whose name was familiar to him. Tearing the cardboard, unscrewing the small cap, he squeezed out some of the contents, smeared it with confidence over his neck and face. Looking up, he saw on the shelves bottles of what he believed to be a cooling and healing extract. He could apply this in the morning and so complete his cure.

Mr. Lecky succeeded in working the large bottle into his coat pocket. Shifting his light inquiringly, he wondered if there were other things he might want or could use to be found here.

Moving on, while he wondered, the dark through which Mr. Lecky's light cut grew more beautiful with scents. Par-

ticles of solid matter so minute, gases so subtle, that they
filtered through stopping and sealing, hung on the un-
stirred air. Drawn in with Mr. Lecky's breath came impalpable dews cooked out of disintegrating coal. Distilled,
chemically split and reformed, they ended in flawless simu-
lation of the aromas of gums, the scent of woods and the
world's flowers. The chemists who made them could do
more than that. Loose on the gloom were perfumes of
flowers which might possibly have bloomed but never had,
and the strong smelling saps of trees either lost or not yet
evolved.

Mixed in the mucus of the pituitary membrane, these
volatile essences meant more than synthetic chemistry to
Mr. Lecky. Their microscopic slime coated the bushed-out
ends of the olfactory nerve; their presence was signalled to
the anterior of the brain's temporal lobe. At once, thought
waited on them, tossing down from the great storehouse of
old images, neglected ideas—sandalwood and roses, musk
and lavender. Mr. Lecky stood still, wrung by pangs as
insistent and unanswerable as hunger. He was prodded by
the unrest of things desired, not had; the surfeit of things
had, not desired. More than anything he could see, or
words, or sounds, these odors made him stupidly aware of
the past. Unable to remember it, whence he was, or where
he had previously been, all that was sweet, impermanent
and gone came back not spoiled by too much truth or exact memory. Volatile as the perfumes, the past stirred him
with longing for what was not—the only beloved beauty
which you will have to see but which you may not keep.

Mr. Lecky's beam of light went through glass top and
side of a counter, displayed bottles of colored liquid—
straw, amber, topaz—threw shadows behind their diverse
shapes. He had no use for perfume. All the distraction, all

the sense of loss and implausible sweetness which he felt was in memory of women.

Behind the counter, Mr. Lecky, curious, took out bottles, sniffed them, examined their elaborately varied forms—transparent squares, triangles, cones, flattened ovals. Some were opaque, jet or blue, rough with embedded metals in intricate design. This great and needless decoration of the flasks which contained it was one strange way to express the inexpressible. Another way was tried in the names put on the bottles. Here words ran the suggestive or symbolic gamut of idealised passion, or festive night, of desired caresses, or of abstractions of the painful allure yet farther fetched. Not even in the hopeful, miracle-craving fancy of those who used the perfumes could a bottle of liquid have any actual magic. Since the buyers at the counters must be human beings, nine of every ten were beyond this or other help. Women, young, but unlovely and unloved, women, whatever they had been, now at the end of it and ruined by years or thickened to caricature by fat, ought to be the ones called to mind by perfume. But they were not. Mr. Lecky held the bottle in his hand a long while, aware of the tenth woman.

Finally he put it down. Picking up his flashlight and turning, he had moved perhaps three steps when, sharp and clear, plainly at the point from which he had first imagined it, broke out the resonant, now nearby, clamor of the bell.

Mr. Lecky jerked his chin. He raised his hands, pressing the palms over his ears, dropped them, moving his head again as though he hoped this sound could be shaken out like loose water. The sharp pealing stopped then, but of itself. He had not done it by either futile measure. Knowing this, his mind was frenzied with his desire for explanation. If, to pay its stubborn poor service, he beat his head with his

fists, the protest must be ineffective; Xerxes whipped the
sea to better purpose. Inappeasable fury to know mounted
the little higher it could; the great tempest of his re-aroused
despair tossed him. It was no longer mental only. He
struck about him with his hands, hitting the air, but that
did not help. Running, he dashed the bottles from the
counter behind. They broke audibly on the floor, spilling
their perfume in pools. At last, in final extravagant spasm,
he hurled his flashlight away. Its shaft turned, undirected,
still shining an instant in the air. It struck then, went out
instantly, leaving him in total darkness.

Mr. Lecky's hand found the counter edge. Moving, his
feet broke again the glass of broken bottles. He stood still,
and the strong smell of synthetic flowers surcharged the
darkness. A quiet slowly followed on the whirlwind. Since
everything had failed—close thought, fury, his folly of
destruction—he must now make failure what he wanted.
Since he could not find the cause, it was time to submit,
content himself with knowing the result.

Mr. Lecky, giving in, no longer insisting on any explanation, had been sorely tried, but contrast would enhance
his reward. Fear could not recrudesce in him; terror could
spur him no further. Fear's many inventions—solitude,
darkness, the chance of enemies prowling in the flesh with
weapons to kill him, the chance of enemies disembodied,
walking his own mind, with the means to drive him mad
—no longer had weight with him. They had not injured or
killed him yet. He was alive. When he moved, it was with
resignation. He did not walk cautiously, for darkness was
nothing to him. He did not listen for enemies. If he met
any it would be time enough to worry about them. He did
not mind being alone; to live, his body was sufficient to itself. What he could not see or explain would have to go
its way, as he now went his.

The climb upstairs was long, but, keeping close to the stair rail, he had no difficulty. On the sixth floor his candle was still burning, a small calm light over the débris of the little explosion. Taking the candle in his hand, Mr. Lecky climbed up to his bed. Yawning, he blew out the flame.

*The architectural limitations of a room are the next consideration. They include its size and proportion, as well as the placement of doors and windows and fireplace. Then there is the style of the decorative treatment to be reckoned with. A fine classic moulding and smooth wall surface demand furniture that is harmonious in feeling. . . .*

No two of the pieces of furniture which had gone to make up Mr. Lecky's fort precisely resembled each other. When Mr. Lecky awoke, lying on his uncomfortable cot, he could see the line of a crazy confusion against the light. Most of the cabinets were not set even or exactly straight. The table, the chair, the cot he lay on, were shoved in carelessly, not arranged.

Work was irksome to Mr. Lecky, but idleness was worse; it was insupportable. Rather than face idleness he could, at least for a while, find things to be done where there was none, and somehow impose on himself the slavery essential to happiness or mere peace. Hopefully he began to find fault with the fort which he had worked so hard to construct. Remembering his harassed inspection yesterday afternoon, it occurred to him that he could, if he chose, set up a new and better establishment in the model rooms across the floor. Without waiting to get himself any breakfast, he was impelled to go at once and see if this were feasible.

Nothing hindered Mr. Lecky's entrance into these apartments but thick velvet cords hooked into rings. He moved

down the row, counting to fourteen. All of them were his
and all the good and interesting things in them awaited
his disposal. There were, for instance, beds of obvious comfort and actual luxuriousness. Mr. Lecky unhooked and let
fall a velvet cord. He was recently enough risen from his
narrow cot to feel satisfaction at such an improvement. He
walked soundless on a carpet taupe-colored and of great
thickness. A canopy overhung the bed-head with the same
flowered percale which hid all but the edges of the woodwork and formed a spread as well. Sitting on the edge of
the bed, Mr. Lecky regarded, less pleased, the walls in old
white. They were painted preciously in an Italian manner
two centuries old to imitate plaster moulding. Pink had
been used. Carrying the scheme to deeper tones, a slipper
chair in cherry-colored satin, an armchair considerably
curved with white painted wood and flowered chintz; a
side chair, at the false window, in red and white stripes had
been added.

Still testing the bed, Mr. Lecky's first objection grew less.
It was founded mainly on his idea of what some imaginary
person, whose scorn he feared, might think of him, if such
were shown to be the room in which he lived. Left to himself, Mr. Lecky found the shape of a chair, the color of
upholstery, a small matter. Well-fitted, strongly fashioned
joints, solid wood, thick padding firmly attached, were the
real virtues. There was an element which he considered
feminine in this room, and he arose, doubtful, resolving to
get himself breakfast before he made any decision.

Downstairs, feeding from the edge of the counter, he
had the litter of previous meals in sight. More work suggested itself to him. Henceforth he could eat in a real
dining-room, with a table and chairs to sit on; and this
greater convenience ought to compensate him for the trouble of carrying up food. He could set about that as soon as

his bedroom was definitely selected and such things as he wanted moved over from his fort.

A second, more thorough investigation showed Mr. Lecky that he might do well to like the bedroom in pink and old white and cherry, the abundant flowering percale. Orchid and pale green and some shades of yellow decorated a room which he considered undoubtedly pretty, but less suitable still. Another supplied twin beds, but he could after all only use one bed.

Returning, thus resolved, to his fort, he set about filling his pack basket once more. He would want his candles and the flashlights, his book. He had also that bottle of witch-hazel extract and the tube of ointment. He had not so much as noticed his burns this morning, but he might as well take his medicines. The witch-hazel, he understood, if needed for no other purpose, could be drunk, producing an agreeable effect. The idea was an irregular and improper one. Drinking it, he was sure, would not be good for him; but his facile curiosity led him to unscrew the cap and taste the contents cautiously. He did not like the flavor, but report was correct. It was drinkable—not too revolting.

Looking now in his lavatory, to see if he had left anything there, he was reminded of the sumptuous bathroom he had looked at yesterday. Distributing the things from his load where they would be handy in the pink room, he turned and went to examine this fine place. As he had more than half foreseen, he found that it was not real. He twitched the faucets one after another, but no water came out their golden mouths. Leaving, disgruntled, he looked around for a washroom to replace the distant one which he had fortified.

Mr. Lecky's discovery that none was nearer displeased

him, expecting, as he did now, every comfort; but since
the need to have protected communication with it was presumably over, he could manage. He stepped into a dining-
room furnished in heavy carved oak and red plush. Sitting
in the monumental chair at the table's head, he rested
while he planned further.

This was the place in which he would like to eat; so a
supply of food enough for several meals ought to be
brought up here. He would need, too, dishes and eating
utensils. Heretofore he had got on well enough without
them, but he did not mean to eat so informally in this fine
and spacious setting. To the disagreeable problem, immediately presented, of washing the things he used he had a
simple solution. He could throw soiled dishes away and
help himself to clean ones from the great stocks on display
on the sixth floor.

Up and down stairs Mr. Lecky passed, bearing his pack
basket. To store his food he made convenient use of the
large double-doored cabinet against the wall. The top of
an oak chest standing under the simulated casement window would serve him for a kitchen. He included the stove
and fuel tins in his next load. In his hands he carried up
several plates and a glass. He was making progress, but
he still had no implements to eat with, aside from his so
variously used kitchen knife, and nothing to cook in. Since
he wanted work to occupy him, he should be glad, for he
knew how much work getting those things would be.


Descending the endless stairs for the sixth time, and as it
was to happen, for the last time of his own will and walking like a free man, Mr. Lecky thought of all the goods
those closed doors hid. Fantastic was the discouragement it
caused him. Aware of such variety and great quantity, Mr.

Lecky saw the danger of forgetting or never even imagining things which, discovered, he would want. Everlastingly midway between two equal errors, to which could he cleave? To have time for everything, one must make haste. To gain access to everything, one must be patient.

Moreover, hasty, or patient as Job, with what great labor would Mr. Lecky carry up on his back all he got! Making, as he was every moment, the climb back longer, giving, as he did with each step down, consent to toil more and more severe, he could anticipate vaguely and abhor another possibility. Curious and insubstantial as his fearing not to find what he could not think of, was his resentment of a perhaps coming time when he might, in revolt against the inanity of exertion, live meanly and miserably, with no object but somehow to make what was already at hand suffice for him. Against this insidious ill chance there exists no defence, since so often what today is detested will appear tomorrow—though surely still detestable—good and wise.

When he had finally, torch in hand, made his way down into the basement, this last sloth of weariness and impairment of too difficult desire was already infecting Mr. Lecky. Walking morosely, brooding in the bad light, he felt no animation in his wish to get silverware or even cooking pots. His dejection might have sent him up empty-handed, had not his indecisive torch beam, sweeping through the thicket of frames—folding wood, strung line, metal rod—on which clothes could be dried after washing, showed him suddenly a pile of oblong packages.

These were lengths of light rope drawn in neat, narrow loops, tightly coiled around, to be used for the same purpose as the frames where space was less constricted. Concerned, discouraged, as Mr. Lecky had been by the thought of endless burdens on his back, he was now refreshed. All was changed by the unexpected, opportune idea. With the

aid of a line he could do his climbing unimpeded and at
the top draw after him fairly heavy loads.

The packages, he learned from the paper encircling
them, contained each twenty yards. With no exact idea, nor
means of forming one, Mr. Lecky guessed that three, or to
be safe, four lengths would be enough. Joined together
they ought certainly to extend from the ninth floor to the
bottom of the stair shaft. He dropped them over his shoulder into the pack basket.

For his kitchen utensils it was necessary to go to those
counters toward the front. Among them, he selected and
added to the rope several sauce pans. A frying pan and a
small kettle he might find occasion to use. Thus laden, he
turned back, went down in the dark and up the stairs by
which he had entered.

Of the things Mr. Lecky had come down to get, only the
silverware for him to eat with remained. Yet, back here,
close to the department in which he had found drugs and
toilet goods, he thought of something else. With the apparent irrelevance of desires not consciously countenanced
making themselves conscious, he recalled his experiment
with the witch-hazel extract. Still sure that it was not
wholesome, feeling too a conviction hard for him to explain, of the enormity of attempting to hearten or warm
himself with a preparation not intended for that purpose,
Mr. Lecky presently found the shelf and took down a second bottle for his pack. Whether he would or would not
drink it, he did not have to settle now. He left the settle-
ment for a time when he might much more greatly desire
to drink it.

Mr. Lecky turned toward the silverware department, and
so toward the stairs in front. This he had planned to do,
and this he was doing; but as he walked, his mind stiff and
discordant in the minor struggle between defiance and

guilt about the bottle, he thought how strangely and frequently he came back to this spot. It was no more than chance, but Mr. Lecky, though he thought nothing of one chance event, could find cause for a grievous and disturbing doubt in chance operating the same way too often.

Able to see the sinister, never-explained bell which must have been the one ringing yesterday, Mr. Lecky began, though vaguely and without concentrated attention, to feel in his mind for a relation of circumstances; and one at least he very soon saw, or thought he did. Nothing would have been more natural than, when the bell rang, for him to go and see what was desired. If he had done that, he would have returned here more times still. Certainly it might be supposed—since now he remembered well having felt it before—that a reason existed for him to come, and some grave instinct, unable to communicate with him logically, worked in this way to overcome his stupidity and blindness, to call his attention to what he must by no means fail to see.

Distressed by his ingenious, uncomfortable idea of something very urgent, momentous, vital, which perhaps he was steadily not seeing, Mr. Lecky stared about him. He even considered inspecting his idiot. So horrid and senseless an impulse he resisted; and, feeling the irrational tug strongly inherent always in gruesome things, he was annoyed. Once annoyed, he saw that the whole matter could be solved by giving himself no more opportunities for fancy. He ought to take care to have no occasion for coming downstairs again for a long time.

Stepping behind a show case and opening it, Mr. Lecky picked up forks, spoons, a knife less dangerous than the one he had been using upstairs; but his resolve to be long coming back suggested a larger supply. Like china, silverware must either be cleaned or discarded. By taking one

of the weighty oblong chests, ostentatiously open inside the
case to show its trays of nested silver pieces, he would supply himself for weeks. It might be difficult to carry so
heavy a load up step by step, but here he could usefully
employ his rope.

Choosing a chest and lugging it to the stair shaft, Mr.
Lecky turned the key in its small lock. Setting down his
basket, he took out a package of rope and fastened one
end to the bar handle set in a plate with sockets on the lid.
For his purpose Mr. Lecky would have found two half
hitches simple and serviceable, but how greatly could trifling matters plague him, for he had never learned to tie
knots properly. What he improvised was a distorted tangle,
an impromptu invention of his own. Tugging it, he considered it satisfactory. Presented next with the need to join
ends, he was inevitably incapable of making a true square
knot, but what he did make again seemed to him all right.
Soon he had four lengths united.

He was, as always, some time in gaining the ninth floor.
Winded, he rested a few minutes, taking the precaution of
fastening the rope end to the rail. Peering over, he could
see the length of it swaying far down to the small chest on
the paving at the bottom. When his breath was recovered,
he began to haul up, hand over hand.

The chest was, to be sure, heavy. The oscillating circle
which it started to describe strained his arms. The moving
rope frayed the skin of his palms. Yet he had lifted it more
than half way, the coils of line accumulating on the floor
beside him, and, encouraged, he pulled faster. A few additional moments, and he might have succeeded; but already
the rope's unlimber newness was stealthily facilitating the
slipping of the second bad knot. Suddenly it ran faster. For
one helpless instant Mr. Lecky could feel the accident impending. The line eased, sprang slightly, swung free. Fall-

ing five stories, the chest landed in an appalling crash of broken wood and scattered silver on stone pavement.

In his indignation, Mr. Lecky stood breathing heavily, more inclined to blame the perversity of the rope than his own now proved ineptitude. Indeed, the failure of his plan seemed to him, as he stood there, to have a possible significance which angered him as much as the accident. He had attempted to get up a chest only because of his determination to insure himself against another descent. Even the fact that he had in his pockets pieces enough for his use, and so needed to go down no more than he intended to, did not wholly reassure him. He lifted up his pack basket mournfully and went into the dining-room. Here he did what he could to forget the matter.

## 8 THE EVENING AT HOME

Mr. Lecky wasted time preparing his dinner, and was in no hurry while he ate it, but he wanted less of it than he had prepared. Attempting to heat a whole tinned chicken, he removed it from its container and put it in a sauce pan, but he was successful in really warming only one side of it. Water had to be fetched from the lavatory and he had filled his kettle full. Over so small and unsteady a flame this was too great a quantity to boil soon. Impatient, he found the powder which boiling water was said to change to coffee unpalatable. These annoyances delayed and inter-

rupted him; but even so, Mr. Lecky had started his meal
too early. When he was done, instead of being night, it
was still late afternoon.

The sunlight, sadly descending, had first to pass the
outer windows. Diluted, it came then through the false
casements of the dining-room. With it were traces of the
original warmth and incomparable glow, but they were
windless, enclosed—heat and light without any life left.
This melancholy illumination reflected up from the table
contributed pallor only to Mr. Lecky's unshaven face. The
slanting shafts, the last sunbeams, barely brought out the
dust motes in the air. Universal silence, not right for day-
time, was impregnate with the inactivity of disuse, vacancy,
human desertion.

To replace the stimulation of crowds and to dispense
with the comforts of human companionship a well-stocked
mind is said to serve. A disordered one probably serves
much better, for few sane men are hermits and few hermits
are very long sane. In any event, Mr. Lecky was without a
well-stocked mind, as he was without further incentive to
action. To clear up the small dreary litter, dispose of the
torn-open cans and the soiled utensils left from the miserable preparation of his dinner would only take a moment.
Having so little to do, Mr. Lecky could see no reason to
start doing it. Instead, he got up, leaving everything. Coming out into the aisle which communicated with his various rooms, he went down to the bedroom. In the extremi-
ties of boredom he often tried reading, had once or twice
found real solace that way.

In the bedroom the more extensive curtains and perhaps
the relative placing of the hidden outside windows made it
almost dark. To read at all, Mr. Lecky would need a light.
Drawing the most comfortable of the chairs close to the
dressing table, he lit two large tapers, placed them erect

and close together by his device of the spilled wax. When their flames had grown full and steadied, he took his book and opened it.

Mr. Lecky read with the careful slowness of a person little given to reading. He read slower even than usual, for the text was difficult and wordy; but on the other hand, he could soon conclude that, even as he had hoped when he saw the indecent jacket, he was sure to find material of some interest. Afraid that he might miss it in this maze of words if he skipped any, Mr. Lecky read doggedly, paragraph by paragraph, page by page.

Perhaps now it was night.

Wondering, Mr. Lecky showed how little this hopeful reading held him. Outside it was as good as dark, and having got up and seen it, he came back; but he did not sit down nor take his book again. He stood bemused, rubbing his chin. Finally he looked at the two bottles on the bureau.

When he reached the dining-room, Mr. Lecky set up and lit another candle. He cleared the remains of his meal away, at least as far as the chest top. Now he had a glass available, but he poured only a little of the liquid from the bottle into it. So little might be supposed to be less harmful, if harm resulted from the drinking. Since none at all would in obvious fact be least harmful, Mr. Lecky was not easy. He smelled it. He tasted it. At last, irresolute, he drank it. This was no sooner done than he regretted the impulse. He stood tense, waiting for it to cause him great pain.

It caused him nothing but a feeling of warmth in his stomach, so after a while, he would seem justified in drinking more, if he wished to, hoping to enjoy greater warmth. Mr. Lecky was not so easily persuaded. That would perhaps be enough for tonight. If no ill came of it, he might,

tomorrow night, try more. He would go back and read a little longer.

Bending forward, Mr. Lecky had been about to blow
out his candle, but it occurred to him that he did not need
to. Light from this source could be squandered; on the
seventh floor he had seen candles in immense quantities.
He might even, if he chose, illuminate several rooms; and
such a plan seemed to him cheerful. He would put candles
in the rooms separating his bedroom from the dining-room.
Thus he had presently an agreeable glow in the too feminine, orchid, green and yellow bedroom, and in a living-
room of some formal elaborateness. The lighting of the
living-room showed him a chair more comfortable than
the one he had been sitting in. If he read again, he would
do it here.

Seated soon in this better chair with his book and the
candlelight arranged to fall on it, Mr. Lecky discovered
one thing not to his liking. If he lifted his eyes they inevitably met a mirror centered over a stiff, slight sofa. At
this angle the glass did not show him himself. Instead, he
saw one lighted edge of the wide-open fourth side of the
room. Dimmer light reached the crowded furniture across
the aisle. More and more indistinct, the angles and edges
of rows behind the first disappeared gradually into a darkness of great depth or extent. Without moving or meaning
to look, Mr. Lecky found himself keeping in this way an
unwanted watch on the night-filled floor. The frame of the
mirror held this view like an important picture; perhaps an
unfinished one whose insignificant and subordinated background was first filled in. It lacked only the thing or person
of which it was intended to be a portrait.

By degrees the vacancy of the mirror took more of Mr.
Lecky's attention than he gave the printed page. He got

up, walked a few steps until he stood opposite the glass. Now the background became the softly lighted wall, and against it he saw himself standing incredulous, for he looked worse than he would have thought, more sinister and unkempt. The mirror, too, attacked his reality, reduced him to a thin image, living, but somehow hardly human, dangerously gross and big in his ill-fitting new suit. This perfect representation would prove to be glass if you advanced and felt it with your fingers. It would prove to be nothing if you stepped a yard aside. The candlelight, up from the table behind, seemed white in reflection, or gray white. Shadows falling forward on Mr. Lecky's face made his eyes look empty and senseless; his face, already soiled with the beard he had begun, was etiolated, exhausted of blood.

No picture was better than one so ugly and disturbing. Restless, Mr. Lecky turned away. He had nowhere to go but to the dining-room, and there he had nothing to do.

This time, Mr. Lecky thought, he must feel better. The dose had been heroic. In his stomach the reddened membranes heated him vitally; his heart drew longer on the beat, squeezed the blood of his life out harder, and so he did feel better. He need not drink any more.

He continued to sit still at the table, for his distracting restlessness was, little by little, becoming dissipated. The longer he sat, the less there remained of it. In its place grew a content, founded not ignobly on mere ease and security, but on slowly and newly felt great reserves of courage and carelessness, reminding him of how relatively well off he was, how much he owned. It made him lordly, positive in his attention, capable of sound quick decisions. After a while he arose, thinking of his book with more relish.

Glancing, as he passed it, at the draped silk and soft colors of the smaller, rejected bedroom, he could notice details not before, nor now, important, but now interesting. His observation was incisive; he saw and liked everything. This bed was made up as though to sleep in. The cover was turned back to show the fine lavender tone of the blankets. They were in turn folded over to show the sheets tinted pale green. An elongated seat or couch, having a support for the back at one end only, was set across the room's far corner. It contained, he saw now, several round satin cushions. Against them lay an ornamental doll with painted face and spineless body, legs angled out under a rich little dress of silk and lace.

The doll pleased Mr. Lecky. Stepping in, he re-arranged it to correct its boneless attitude of soft exhaustion. Seeing it set up, he liked it better immodestly prostrated, as it had first been, and touched it back. Now he examined the walls and was taken at once by an unnoticed trio of oval, terra-cotta masks affixed as decorations. Light from the big candle he had placed on the dressing table shone on their glazed surfaces; but under that their broad blunt features were warm-colored. They looked out narrow-eyed, drowsy, as though hung up still in a languor from some sustained obscenities.

But, alas, the fronts of faces only, as the beautiful debauched doll was only stuffed cloth.

Mr. Lecky sat on the edge of the bed a moment, staring back at them. Fancy, considering them, was freer here. The complicated art of reading did not interrupt. Mr. Lecky thought with clarity of women, whole and actual.

More real in this use than any exactly named or definitely remembered face was the immense store of impressions, the glimpses, the aggregation of numberless forgotten or unnoticed turns of desire when unchastened fancy wasted its minute on a wish too sudden and untimely for possible fulfillment.

Mr. Lecky sat there on the ornate, to him, beautiful, bed, a hand resting on the turned-back sheets, relishing the suggestion that some woman would presently retire to this expensive room and go to bed. Imagining what she might look like, he suffered from the surfeit of faces he would like her to have—none could be too high or too low, none too beautiful or too scornful.

Once fitted to this intimacy, the color of eyes, the tones of hair, individual details of expression, of speech or gesture, he could make free with all women, find in them all a charm not airy like the word and trifling, but rank and vital, sinking through his warm breast, rooted in the quick, fed on the sap of his bowels where the alcohol inflamed them. In this happy stupor he brooded over his imaginary guests, undressing. Their individual deft ways of slipping off a stocking, or stepping out of a dress, absorbed him. He saw the candlelight and the shadows on their serene bare flesh before they re-clothed themselves to sleep. One followed another; they arrived with grace and he observed them. They took down their hair, if they had hair possible to take down, did whatever they considered necessary with the toilet articles spread out on the bright dressing table, slipped into bed; slept, he could presume.

> . . . *we easily know*
> *By this these angels from an evil sprite*
> *Those set our hairs, but these our flesh upright.*

Time was passing over him, and with its passing Mr. Lecky felt a faraway numbness. Slowly, do what he would, he was forgetting these women, he was disinclined to con-

centrate. Arising, he went back to the table in the dining-
room and filled his glass.

Movement, or more drink, seemed to restore, though in
a mood altogether passive, the earlier acuteness of thought
and feeling. Creeping up on Mr. Lecky, seeping up from
his stomach, came the fine awareness of a horizon enlarged.
Less graphic, this mood took away his need to stir himself
or find anything to do. He was happy merely to sit there
in the dining-room with his glass. He was calmed by the
freedom and meditative scope of tranquil distances. At
peace in his seat, at peace he could be, too, in a whole imaginary realm where he had access, effortless and unlimited.
What this kingdom contained that was so valuable he did
not have to know. Indeed, it contained nothing which
could be known; it was formed entirely of undefined possibilities. Named, or in any way pushed toward fact, they
would cease to exist. To Mr. Lecky, drinking, it seemed
very likely that henceforth, from this time on, he would
have the intelligence to live here. He would not allow himself to return to the disappointing past, nor submit to any
detestable present.

This was such a good thing, coming indubitably out of
his glass, that more drink ought to bring him things even
better. Anxious to enjoy them, Mr. Lecky reached for the
bottle. Pouring, he spilled a little, for he was very drunk.

## 9 THE FAMILIAR FACE

Sometime Mr. Lecky had left the dining-room. The candles had burned themselves to flat pools in which the last fragments of the wicks fell over and drowned. Starting to remove his clothes to go to bed, Mr. Lecky had never finished, and though he slept profoundly, he did not sleep at ease.

Coming to consciousness he was afflicted by an immense misery of pain and sickness. Though he had not slept long, he had drunk late, so there was a gloom of day, sullen, without sun. His distress hardly let him think, but such dreariness might mean rain outdoors.

Mr. Lecky lay motionless; the misery of his body absorbed him. He might, he supposed, feel better soon. He could lie quiet, probably sleep.

Now that he thought of seeking it again, he did not like sleep. Relinquishing himself to that nothingness, though safely done ten thousand times, had never convinced him. It was always too much like death, and more like it than ever now. The laboring ill-ease that woke him up remained. A subconsciousness, a kind of fibered awareness, let him feel his physical being, travailing and heavy laden, doing all it could.

Feeling this, it was possible to feel deeply if not clearly how little more might be too much. All the amazing resources, the infinite, sensitive and skillful compensations, the incredible faculties for repair, would prove too slow or

too minute. There would be a last frantic effort, an em-
bargo on the wasted energy of consciousness. In this coma,
matters would go, however, from bad to worse. Even indis-
pensable processes must slow and stop. Perhaps there
would be a moment's complete halt, an utter end to activity; but most cells would be for a long while still living,
ignorant of the disaster until the hectic microscopic carni-
val of decay burst in on them. Only bones would be left
when this concluding liveliness was ended.

Mr. Lecky, well enough, if unwillingly, aware of the rot
sometime awaiting him, was disgusted to think of his good
flesh so reduced. The certainty of its end made it prema-
turely loathsome. It was foul stuff—wretched man, to be
so amply provided with it! It was the means of his horrid
predestination. It consigned Mr. Lecky to the extinction
he abhorred; it marked him, still living, for putrefaction.
Who should deliver him from the body of this death?

Mr. Lecky suffered, with the thought of his end, the
stripping of himself to solitude. Here he developed nothing;
he only saw what he had. His isolation in skull and breast
had advanced with his unfolding in the womb. Before there
was a consciousness to be incarcerated, its prison was built.
There separate and single-handed consciousness grew up.
For cold comfort Mr. Lecky could have the assurance that
no man was lonelier or less lonely than any other, than himself. From his terrible fastness, Mr. Lecky signalled, a
doubtful solace, with his voice. Back over a void more absolute than the width of the world came to his ears the faint
halloos in kind. Locked up for life, he had not life, no
friends, no servant but his slovenly body. Humbled by
thought, Mr. Lecky might see himself as only the whole
shadow, sum of those part shadows, his past years; but seen
by others, the whole of him came to less. All of him there
was could be found in the industrious fomenting cesspool

of his guts, the oxidation sack of lungs and appended heart, the cavity packed with a few pounds of the soft moist protoplasmic mass of his brain. Whatever their lonely efforts, like children making playmates of trees and rocks, his fellow men at most imagined themselves in him, did to him as they would be done by. In ultimate fact, they were completely and helplessly indifferent. They passed by on the other side. Looking over, if they did, they saw Mr. Lecky, too, passing; him, too, remote, deep in himself, indifferent.

On the wide bed, Mr. Lecky, gross and dishevelled, stirred moaning, put his hands on the mattress, half pushing himself up. He thought of going to his lavatory; but even as he moved, shaky with pain and illness, he heard an intolerable well-known sound far away in the store.

> *Deliver me from mine enemies, O God:*
> *defend me from them that rise up against me.*
> *Deliver me from the workers of iniquity,*
> *and save me from the bloody men.*

Desiring to keep him in where he could rest and at leisure realise his misery, his hopelessness, the great terror of being where he was, Mr. Lecky's mind resisted somewhat.

Yet, staggering to his feet, he passed groaning down the line of his rooms. Out he went by the stair door. His perfidious body conveyed him; it was, as he had always known, his enemy. This personal Judas, gone to the adversary, took everything. Mr. Lecky was left with no means to quit himself like a man. He had no feet to plant, no muscles to tug back, no hands to catch at passing holds.

He had no body to sweat and quake, no superfluous saliva to swallow. He held the rail of the stairs, fearing that terrible fall; and quickly, step by step, he reduced it.

Now he put behind him, toys, games, sporting goods, musical instruments, cameras. This was the eighth floor.

Rugs and carpets, upholstery fabrics, pillows, curtains, lamps, pictures, pottery, clocks. This was the seventh floor.

Groceries, glassware, china, table furnishings.

Men's wear, men's shoes, luggage, smoking supplies.

Boys', girls', and infants' apparel, baby carriages, nursery furniture. (He left no heirs of his body.)

Lingerie, negligees, corsets, cotton frocks, house dresses, women's and misses' outer apparel, furs. (His bed was empty, his house untended.)

Thrusting his face over the rail, Mr. Lecky saw that he would not fall far, if he fell, but he hastened. He did not wish to fall at all; and so he came out while the bell still rang. In the gloom of the dark day he could see the pale illuminated spark of its breaking circuit high on the pillar.

Now, under the bell, Mr. Lecky stopped, for the great gloom was deeper, and how could it be evening yet? From his pocket, thoughtless, he took his watch, looking at it lying in his hand. Still it said quarter past five; but as he would have put it back, remembering, he saw that it was going. The second hand progressed, marching its round, numbering the moments. In the dusk fallen at what he thought was noon, Mr. Lecky began to shake, while the bell sounded stridently on, peal after peal.

Who could be deaf to such ringing?

Mr. Lecky waited, and while his eyes ached in the gloom, he knew that no one could be; he heard that no one was.

Heavy the labor of climbing, awful the need to learn who went there, who rang, who must be met half way! When you are dead it is hard to stand on your feet, to climb stairs, to keep your slit throat together; yet how that last was done Mr. Lecky now found out. You hold a hand upon your face to steady your head, and one upon your throat to close it, and step by step, you crawl until the top is reached and you can lie forward there.

Clutching the watch tight, Mr. Lecky, creeping too, drew near. He stooped. Unwillingly, he took the idiot by the shoulder. Crouching as he turned up the fearful face, he bent his own face toward it, saw it again. His hand on the head, studying the uninjured side, Mr. Lecky beheld its familiar strangeness—not like a stranger's face, and yet it was no friend's face, nor the face of anyone he had ever met.

What this could mean held him, bent closer, questioning in the gloom; and suddenly his hand let go the watch, for Mr. Lecky knew why he had never seen a man with this face. He knew who had been pursued and cruelly killed, who was now dead and would never climb more stairs. He knew why Mr. Lecky could never have for his own the stock of this great store.